A Novel by:

Baron R. Birtcher

Library of Congress Cataloging-in-Publication Data
Birtcher, Baron, 1959-

Roadhouse Blues / by Baron Birtcher

Library of Congress Catalog Card Number: 00-105932

p. cm.

ISBN 1-930754-00-0

First Edition

10 9 8 7 6 5 4 3 2 1

Visit our Web site at
http://www.durbanhouse.com

This book is dedicated to
Christina, the love of my life
and
Allegra, Raider and Britton,
my greatest treasures

ACKNOWLEDGMENTS

My sincere thanks go out to my childhood pal, and police detective, Mark Simon. He patiently talked me through some of the finer points of police procedure, and any mistakes or misstatements in that regard are purely mine. To John Lewis of Durban House for his dedication, perseverance and direction. Thank you for your leadership. Sofia Shafquat for her editorial help.

Christina, I could have never finished without your encouragement and belief in me. Thanks for reading all those early drafts, and for being kind with your criticism. You are the love of my life. And to my son, Raider, who asked me every day how it was coming along. It meant the world to me.

Thanks to Nancy and Mark Miller for a million and a half copies, alot of great vibes and a really cool logo. You guys are the best, and mahalo nui for all the aloha and oleo paipai. And to Angie Faini for her help in organizing all the word processing files.

Thanks to Dave and Rosalie Fink for big-kine encouragement and great times on land and under water "and the whole Mary Anne." And to Jacquie and Kurt Whitney. Thanks for the names.

None of this would have happened if my grandfather, F.E. Birtcher, hadn't taught me to believe that I could do anything I put my mind to. My time to know you was far too short, but the mark you've left on so many lives keeps you near always. Me ke aloha pumehana.

Prologue

Olympic Park
Los Angeles, 1983

"HAVE YOU MADE UP YOUR MIND?" THE OLD WOMAN asked, watching the face of the young woman seated on the bench beside her.

"Yes," the younger one said. The tension in her face vanished.

"You are sure?" There was no room for missteps. Too much was at stake.

The young blonde stared after the boy as he fed the ducks at the edge of the pond. A breeze ruffled his curly brown hair. She nodded.

"Then you have to tell the boy."

"I'll tell him," she answered too quickly. She regretted her tone immediately.

The old woman persisted. "He has to begin before he reaches puberty."

"I'll tell him."

"You know there is only one," the old woman said as she placed her palm on a thick parcel in plain brown wrapping laying on the bench.

"I understand." She knew this very well.

"In any generation there is only one."

"I remember." She responded more patiently this time. "I'll tell the boy."

* * *

*THE club was thick with it, that mix of sex and recklessness and waiting for the West Coast's reigning rock idols, the Doors. It was a private listening party that heightened the rut, knocking down barriers, for the newest, as-yet-unreleased album, **L.A. Woman.***

The slender young blonde had become a regular in recent months, making acquaintances and praying for an invitation like this. It was a hell of a long way from Indianapolis. Yet here she was. An exclusive soiree in one of the hottest nightspots on the Sunset Strip.

1970 was going to be her year.

Kelsey gently stroked the tiny bubbles of condensation from her glass, following her own sensual movements with moss-green eyes. She felt the club's closeness. Thick rich, pungent smoke permeated her skin, hair, and clothing. Behind a lazy smile, the young woman's mind wandered freely with a high that felt as if she could hear the very breath of strangers. Through the din, she could perceive their thoughts, see their emotions.

She felt the crackling energy on her skin. It was starting.

Morrison was in the room. An undulation of pressing bodies.

Kelsey floated in it all, just an insignificant drop in a kalei-doscopic sea of long hair, paisley shirts, pinstriped pants, mul-ticolored beads, and fringed leather jackets. The regular cult of Whisky A-Go-Go freaks: Vito, Carl and the rest of their crowd. Vito and Carl, both over forty, screaming to fit the scene with their outrageous costumes of brightly colored tights, capes and leotards. Their presence imprinted all major events at the club.

No one was choosing to remember the times when the Doors had been banned from playing there. Lewdness, the authori-ties had said at the time. Now they were welcoming the band back like they were some sort of royalty.

Hypocrites, Kelsey thought, her thumb smearing down the glass.

She had never seen anyone as charismatic, as completely sexual, as Jim Morrison. Never. She had been introduced to him once, back stage after a concert. He had been so coked-out at the time she was sure that he didn't even remember her, but her fantasy lived on, and ignited an inner fire. He had even looked into her eyes, smiled, and repeated her name like a line of poetry.

Her reverie was interrupted by her tablemate, Judy.

"Hello...Hello.....!" Judy said, waving her hands in an exag-gerated attempt to get Kelsey's attention. "Jesus, Kel, are you even seeing this? It's in-fucking-credible! I can't believe the vibe here!"

"Unbelievable. Yeah." Her glass rotated between her fin-gers, bubbles rising, dying.

The marijuana she and Judy had smoked earlier was now taking its toll on her. SLO - MO - SHUN. Not scary or any-

thing, just time elongated, feeling she could see every moment of her passing life.

The Jack Daniels and Coke was luke warm as she felt it slide down her throat. Its warm comfort mixed with the euphoric feelings left behind by the grass and the snort of blow she had been given in the women's bathroom.

"My God," Kelsey's words caromed across to Judy. "It can't get any better than this."

"Out of sight," Judy shouted back, raising her beer in a pantomime of a toast.

The first loud strains of guitar and bass thumped into her chest.

A prominent local deejay announced, "Ladies and gentlemen, I give you..... the Doors!"

A thunderstorm of applause and whistles nearly drowned out the music.

The stage stood empty but for two tall stacks of black speaker boxes, a chrome stalk of microphone stand, and an enormous mural of the Doors that hung as a backdrop running the entire length of the stage. Jim Morrison's eyes seemed alive, captured brilliantly by the artist.

Kelsey turned to Judy, smiled widely, then stood so as to completely give herself over to the music, to let herself get lost in Morrison's sensuous, smoky voice:

> ".....Are you a lucky little lady in the City of Light
> Or just another lost angel
> City of Night
> City of Night
> City of Night ...."

Vibrating shouts and applause rose like an incoming tide before the album's next track. Kelsey had to stand on her toes to see the stage. The four band members snaked their way through the crowd for the high ground afforded by the small stage. They were back. A victory. A celebration of early day performances.

Tonight, though, the group was not there to perform. This major force in rock music was celebrating the completion of their newest album. "Erotic Politicians", Jim Morrison had once proclaimed themselves.

The band ascended the stage amid the ovation. Each musician was in character: John Densmore looked wary and vaguely uncomfortable with the whole scene; Ray Manzarek cool and scholarly; Robbie Kreiger somewhat detached and shy. And then there was Morrison, who looked every bit the poet: tortured, beautiful, sinister and sensuous. A god.

The Doors stood shoulder to shoulder on the stage, Manzerek blowing a kiss to his pretty wife, who stood at the rear of the room surrounded by record label people and hangers-on. Morrison's face held the curious look of a man who was studying the faces in the audience as if from inside a cage. He made eye contact with Kelsey, sending a spontaneous sexual thrill through her core. She shivered involuntarily. Then his eyes moved on, almost predatory.

The occasion was thrillingly without precedent in Kelsey's short life, a wayward California "hippie," late of Indianapolis, Indiana. She felt the throb of music touch her again and rejoined Judy and the roiling crowds. Moving with the music Kelsey undulated on whiskey, grass and cocaine. She could fly if she wanted to.

A hand entered her world, firm and warm upon her shoulder.

Hot, whiskey-laced breath at her ear and neck. Without turning around, Kelsey closed her eyes and leaned into the presence that had closed in behind her.

Morrison pressed his lips close. She shivered again.

He whispered, "Why don't you and I get outta this place?"

Nothing could have diminished the overwhelming desire to follow Jim wherever he led. She let him take her hand in his and weave their way to the back door. She knew, she knew she would fly with God.

The limo maneuvered smoothly through the busy late night traffic that led from the Whisky to the small hotel where Morrison was living, just off of La Cienega. The ride was brief. After easing the car to the curb, the driver hastily appeared at the rear door of the long vehicle and opened it.

* * *

Morrison's second-floor room was dingy and stale, permeated with the smell of whiskey and beer. It carried Jim's musk.

The flashing red and blue of an outdoor sign dimly suffused the room, filtering through flimsy curtains. Desultory shadows moved on the mostly empty walls.

Jim strode to a cupboard in the kitchenette and took a quart of Jack Daniels, unscrewed the cap and lifted it to his lips for a long pull. He swallowed hard, then held the bottle at arm's length to her.

She took it and drank deeply, too.

He smiled, predatory eyes now quiet. Morrison staggered toward a small box sitting on a narrow ledge that protruded from the wall. He picked it up in one hand while gripping the neck of the quart of brown bourbon in the other. The box was black lacquer with intricate oriental designs around the borders of the lid. He overturned it on the coffee table. Kelsey sat on the frayed sofa and watched the cascade of white powder.

Morrison dragged the edge of a razor back and forth across the glass tabletop until several long, straight lines of cocaine appeared. He produced two short bamboo straws, handed one to Kelsey and kept the other. He held his straw almost daintily between his thumb and forefinger, lifted it to his nostril, and took a deep drag. Morrison closed his eyes, and laughed aloud, throaty and low.

Kelsey leaned toward the remaining line, snorted, then laughed with him in shared pleasure. She lit a pair of red candles that stood on his mantel, then returned to the coffee table to repeat their shared ritual with the white powder and whiskey until both were nearly gone.

Candlelight flickered off the white walls and ceiling of the drab room. It offered a ghostly visual dance to the music that now played on the room's cheap stereo. Kelsey's soul was floating. Free of her body, her essence circled the passing moments unfolding in the room. Far, far away she flew with her young god, propelled by earthly passion.

He reached to her and placed his hand behind her head, pulling her gently but firmly toward him. She made no effort to resist, and let him guide her to his warm lips. He leaned his face to hers, and she gave herself, opening her mouth to the exploring oneness of his deep kiss.

Without speaking, they lowered themselves to the floor   He found the back of her neck and kissed the velvet skin. He discovered the heat of her beneath the loose, white cotton blouse. Morrison pulled her on top of him. Kelsey willingly followed his lead, spreading her legs.

He lifted the blouse over her head, revealing taut, pink nipples. Arching her back, she leaned her firm breasts into his waiting lips and eased her thumbs beneath the waistband of her jeans. She raised up on her knees, and pushed them down over slender hips.

Kelsey couldn't wait to feel him inside of her. She moved on languid limbs to reveal him, a totem in her hands, as her legs wishboned him. Pushing, panting, riding the rising storm, she felt herself burst. Her head felt light, then she fell against his heaving chest, her hair wet and falling across his face. Pale yellow flames. Glowing bodies. Perspiration offering up a golden luminescence.

It was as if she could feel the new life begin inside of her, this moment of moments, even while she was still in his arms.

Chapter One

I CAREFULLY ROLLED MY SIX-FOOT-ONE INCH frame out of my generous bed in the master stateroom of my sailing yacht, the *Kehau,* doing my best not to wake my guest, the twenty-two-year-old daughter of this week's charter customers. Tiffany's parents had taken a two-day deep sea fishing expedition that I had set up with a friend of mine, and she had opted to stay behind. So sue me.

I was reminded of my earlier attention to care and safety in this day and age when I stepped noisily on the wrapper of last night's condom. Still, she didn't wake. Her strawberry hair spilled across the pillowcase, and the look of youthful content ignited in me a fleeting jealousy of the peaceful sleep that I could no longer access. Twenty years "on the Job" had seen to that.

Out of habit, I checked the Beretta automatic stashed in the drawer beside the bed, then made my way to the galley to heat up some hot water for my morning cup of herbal tea. Mike Travis, caffeine-free superhero for a new millennium.

At 5:45 on a Saturday morning, it was already topping seventy degrees. Another warm morning in Avalon. The last one in June. While I filled the glass teapot with bottled water from the refrigerator, I casually surveyed the harbor to see if any new boats had arrived during the night. The only thing that caught my eye was the thin, orange line that underscored the buttermilk ripples of clouds to the east, over the mainland. No matter where I found myself, it pacified me to catch the first light of day. So much death. So much darkness. The sunrise was my talisman.

Avalon is a small resort town, about a mile square in size. The harbor that borders it has only about fifty moorings, and I was fortunate that my family's long, local history had helped me secure one of them.

Tall palms lined the shore, sprouting from large planters ornately decorated with Spanish tile. Each marked the point of intersection of several modest sidestreets with Crescent Avenue, the comparatively wide and busy main boulevard that traced the gentle curve of the harbor's shoreline.

In winter, the town was a sleepy, seaside hideaway, vastly different in pace and attitude from the congested cities that ran along the western shore of the southern California mainland, only about twenty five miles east. Every summer, though, Avalon became a bustling resort, teeming with tourists seeking the charm of a quaint village reminiscent of the Mediterranean, but accessible by helicopter, plane or boat in a matter of minutes.

World class scuba diving and deep-sea fishing were also considerable sources of visitor activity, and dive charters aboard my yacht were the main source of my income since retiring from the LAPD's Homicide bureau.

After starting the burner beneath the teapot, I padded across the plush, deep green carpeting of the salon to find an appropriate CD to provide the soundtrack for the morning. The sea was glassy, and reflected the morning's colors like an undulating, misshapen mirror.

I thumbed through the drawer beneath my built-in stereo, a custom designed Bang and Olufson component system, and finally decided on Craig Chaquiso's *Acoustic Highway*. By the time I had set the volume and adjusted the speakers to play only outside on the aft deck, careful to avoid disturbing Tiffany's worry-free slumber, the teapot was boiling and ready for me. Mango Ceylon.

As I blew at the steam rising from the cup, a vague melancholy took me. Odd and random recollections from my former life flashed through my mind and left remnants, like vapor trails, that I could feel but could not hold onto. In a way, I had set myself adrift from a job that had once consumed nearly every moment of my life and had traded it for a freedom so complete that it hadn't yet filled the hollow space that was left behind.

I didn't mind. I knew it would take time to adjust, but it took a certain resolve. I desperately wanted to blot out the sickness, abuse, torture and violent death I had witnessed for so many years. I had stared into the darkness long enough to feel it begin to take root inside me, but I couldn't allow it.

So I changed my life. Moved to the peace of a small town and the liberation of the sea.

I closed my eyes, took a deep breath, and let the salt air bring me back to reality.

With my feet propped up on the aft rail, the cool leather of the deck chair underneath me and the steaming cup in my hand, I returned to security in the belief that today would be just fine. It had to be, or what the hell was it all for?

That's when the VHF radio crackled to life.

"Hey, Mike, you awake?"

I always left the VHF on just in case of emergency.

I knew it was Art at the pier, and there was no reason to pretend I hadn't heard him. He had already seen me through his Bushnell binoculars, and was probably looking at me with the glasses in one hand and the radio's microphone in the other at that very moment. Lots of privacy on one's yacht here in Avalon.

"Yeah, Art, I'm up," I answered.

"Mind if I come out in a couple minutes, I've got something here that just came in for you."

Art is with the Harbor Patrol, having spent most of his thirty year career with the Los Angeles Sheriff's Office in Avalon, doing pretty much what he was doing now. LASO runs the Harbor Patrol. Though I had done my twenty with the LAPD, Art thought of the two of us as something like comrades-in-arms. Except I was now retired at the youthful age of forty-one.

Art liked to come around in the slow hours of the day to have some coffee, which he always called a "cuppa Joe." Too many Dashiell Hammett novels, I guess. We would trade cop stories, with the majority of the air time being devoted to his asking me about my experiences in Homicide.

I run my seventy-two foot, custom-built, blue-water sailing yacht as an occasional sailing and scuba charter, allowing me enough money and time to pretty much choose where I go and what I do without dipping into the trust fund that my father had set up for my brother and me before he died six years ago. What my persion doesn't cover, the occasional charter makes up.

"Well...uh, Art, I have a guest aboard...." I answered back, opting for discretion and subtlety over the open airwaves.

"No problem. I'll be right out." So much for being indirect.

Within moments, I saw Art's stocky silhouette climb into the twenty-one foot Mako center-console boat that the Harbor Patrol used for tooling about the harbor, and heard the engine start. It was the only sound in that warm, quiet morning, besides the rhythmic lapping of small waves against my boat. Three minutes later, Art, empty plastic coffee mug in hand, was side-tying to the *Kehau* wearing his uniform of khaki shorts, shirt, badge, and shit-eating grin.

"What?" I asked after he had ascended the ladder from his skiff to my afterdeck.

"I got a message for you. From the mainland. You're supposed to page Hans from your old office." The smile was getting wider.

"Well......what's it about?"

"Don't know. They said you should oughta call 'em back on a land line. Not cellular. They said to make sure and tell you 'not cellular'. " If the grin got any wider, his ears were going to meet in the back of his head.

"Great. Well, like I said, I have a guest aboard, and it'll have to wait 'til later, Art. And anyway, I'd have to use your office phone if they want me to use a land line."

"No worries. I wrote the number on my desk blotter. You go ahead and take the Mako to my office, and I'll wait here. They told me it was important that you call right away. Just let me know what's what when you get back, all right?" He was obviously hoping to be on the receiving end of another great cop story.

A few minutes later, as I pulled the Harbor Patrol Mako away from my yacht, I watched Art rummaging purposefully through my galley preparing his morning "cuppa Joe."

*   *   *

I HAVE to admit that I was curious as hell about the call. I have heard from my former partner, Hans Yamaguchi, exactly twice since I left Homicide. Once at my retirement party, and once when I threw my own boat-launching for the *Kehau,* over a year ago.

Hans is an interesting guy. His father is Japanese, his mother German. A one-man Axis. He is fortunate to have garnered the best of both cultures and genetics with thick black, short cropped hair, a quick mind, and a lean, muscular physique. At nearly six feet and one hundred and ninety pounds, he is in as good condition as a man fifteen years younger, a fact he attributes to a daily regimen of exercise, mainly consisting of free weights and martial arts.

His square face has the ability to appear expressionless in nearly any situation. Dark Occidental eyes only occasionally betray his deepest thoughts. This latter fact I had learned the hard way some years ago. For years, we had been not only partners in Homicide, but had made worthy competitors mastering the mental and physical disciplines of Aikido.

And we had grown to become friends, at least until I had somehow distanced myself from nearly everyone from the old days. From the Job. I didn't want to carry that weight anymore, and I didn't know how to put it behind me without closing the door on all of it. On everyone.

I punched in Hans' pager number on the Harbor Patrol's land line which Art had written down. After three rings, a disembodied voice asked that I please enter the number from which I was calling, followed by the pound sign. I did as I was instructed, and waited for the call to be returned.

In less than five minutes, the phone in front of me rang.

I picked up, and before I could speak, I heard a familiar voice intone, "Yamaguchi. I was just paged."

A cop will regularly give his pager number to confidential informants. He wasn't going to volunteer any information unnecessarily.

"Hans, this is Mike."

No response.

"Travis," I added.

 Still no response.

"Mike Travis," I said again, like I was practicing my own name.

"Yeah.... right ....uh... Mike, we've got a call-out here that looks like you could be of some help on," he answered cryptically.

I waited for more, but nothing came.

My thoughts scattered around still instinctual reactions. There was a familiar surge of adrenaline, but it was tempered by a new weariness. Something in my bones. So much for the youthful age of forty-one. I wanted my Mango Ceylon and all the Tiffanys that might cross my wake. I wanted quiet Avalon mornings and dappled reflections of buttermilk sunrises.

My dry throat closed down.

"I've got a chopper on its way to pick you up now. Should be there in....." Hans paused momentarily, " ...twenty-two

minutes." He hung up.
Fuck.

Chapter Two

THE BELL JET RANGER LANDED ON THE ROOFTOP of a squat municipal building adjacent to Union Station, Los Angeles' landmark train depot. The trip was thirty minutes of vibration and noise from the small heliport on the extreme east end of Catalina. A uniformed patrolman was there to transport me to the crime scene.

As the rotor blades wound down, the officer reflexively hunched under them and opened the passenger door. He looked extremely young, complete with razor-cut brown hair, and that expectant look of a new uniformed cop.

"Mister Travis?" he confirmed as he extended his hand in greeting.

"That's right."

We had to shout over the throbbing noise of the chopper.

"I'm Pete Bartok. It's an honor to meet you. The dicks sent me to bring you to the scene. Detectives Yamaguchi and Kemp are there now."

He walked in front of me toward the double glass doors on the rooftop landing pad and held one of them open for me to pass through. We took the stairs down to the first-level basement parking area where several Los Angeles city vehicles were parked, including a couple of patrol cars.

"That one," the officer said as he pointed to the black-and-white farthest from us.

It had been a while since I sat in a patrol car, but there is something about the smell. They all smell the same, and it really took me back. A combination of hot vinyl seats, cigarette smoke, sweat and cheap cologne.

As we corkscrewed our way to street level, Bartok radioed ahead that we were on our way.

"They teach some of your cases at the Academy," he offered after a long silence. "It's great to meet you in person."

"Hmmm." I gazed absently out the window. This was a conversation I could hardly wait not to have.

"How long were you in, twenty?"

"Yep." Jesus. Take a hint.

"I want to get Homicide some day," he enthused.

You and everybody else, I thought.

"Good luck then," I said out loud. *I hope you enjoy the bodies. Especially the ones that crowd your dreams.*

We crawled up the on-ramp toward the slow, mechanical crush of the freeway and it fell around me like a yoke. I was wondering for the hundredth time what I was doing here and I hoped amid the radio chatter that the young officer would keep quiet.

"So, how'd *you* get there? Into Homicide, I mean."

He was like that piece of corn that gets stuck in your teeth.

"I spent five years in a radio car. One day my sergeant asked me if I wanted to work a drug investigation. He told me they wanted me for an undercover assignment."

What that really meant was that I got to walk the seedy streets of a rundown neighborhood, looking and smelling like a wino, pushing a shopping cart full of empty aluminum cans and assorted garbage.

"Yeah?" Bartok prompted. "What was your cover?"

"Homeless drunk."

"Mmmm." He was disappointed. He expected *Miami Vice*.

"The occupant of the house we were watching was a mid-level coke dealer. I figured since I was supposed to be a wino, I might as well dig through the guy's trash cans. I came across some phone bills he'd tossed and they led to the ID of his supply and distribution connections." No one ever said that criminals were smart.

"So then what happened?" I was in the middle of my own documentary.

"Working that detail got me noticed, and six months later I was promoted to Detective. My first assignment was a couple of years in Sex Crimes. From Sex Crimes, I went over to Narcotics. From there to Homicide."

And from Homicide to retirement. Until this morning.

We finally pulled out onto the 101 Freeway heading north, and immediately became part of the ever-present L.A. traffic. Glaciers move faster.

I pulled out my cell phone and called Art at Harbor Patrol. After pressing me for details I couldn't yet provide on why I'd been called to L.A., he confirmed that my buddy Rex had gone over to the *Kehau* to look after my charter until I got back.

"Where are we going?" I asked the young cop after a welcome silence.

"Venice. Down by the pier."

That didn't shock me. There is rarely a shortage of bizarre behavior down there.

Another 40 minutes and we arrived at the crime scene, a sizable area bounded by bright-yellow tape marked CRIME SCENE in thick black letters. That was in case you couldn't tell what it was by the number of patrol cars, flashing lights, ambulance, coroner's vans, photographers, reporters, and various lookers-on.

It was close to 7:30 in the morning, and I was about to get a look at the first murder victim I had seen in well over a year.

*   *   *

THE body was surrounded by a hive of activity.

The ID tech was completing the process of photographing the victim. Detectives Hans Yamaguchi and Dan Kemp looked on. Coroner's investigators and criminalists were scouring the area for any bits of forensic evidence that might be found, most of them working with sifters, examining the leftovers as the sand filtered through the mesh. There were two others with metal detectors. A sandy beach was not going to be an easy place to find anything of much use on the case, but they'd use every crime scene investigative process nevertheless.

I checked in with the uniformed officer in charge of the crime scene, and was directed toward a narrow, well-worn path of packed sand that led to the body. The trail had been meticulously sifted, searched and studied, had yielded nothing of forensic value, and now served as the only route I could take without possibly disturbing undiscovered evidence.

Hans was on his haunches with his back toward me, so Kemp saw me first.

"Well, if it isn't L.A.'s own Hawaiian yachtsman," he said.

"Fuck you, Kemp." It came out easily, picking up right where I had left off with him when I left the job. It was common departmental knowledge that Dan had gotten his detective's shield because his uncle had some sort of pull with an influential city councilman. He had kissed ass all the way up through the ranks to Homicide.

Hans turned then. His mouth was a tight straight line; only his eyes registered anything resembling welcome.

"Hey, Mike. Glad you're here. The 'crim' is almost done, so you're just in time to watch Dan here oversee the collection of prints." He got to his feet.

"Hey, Hans." I extended my hand to him. "You sure you don't want someone more qualified to do it?"

"Don't fucking start," he said to both Kemp and me.

Kemp was red-faced. I just smiled.

"What you've missed so far," Hans went on, flipping open his case notes, "is this: kid surfer, name of Jeff Burnett, finishes surfing, walks across the sand under the pier on the way to his car, and damn near trips over Jane here." Hans used the "Jane Doe" for the as-yet-unidentified victim.

He continued, "Surfer takes a closer look, as she's wearing only panties and T-shirt, determines that the bluish tint of the skin is weird even by Venice standards, and comes to the conclusion that she's dead. He drops the surfboard he's carrying, gets down on all fours, and pukes all over the sand.

"When he's finished crapping up our crime scene, he finally stands and drags — yes drags — the goddamn surfboard all the way over to the street where you just came from, wiping out whatever other useful things we might find vis-s-à-vis our killer. It's an obvious body dump, since her lividity is out of whack with body position."

I nodded my agreement with Hans' assessment, then craned my neck to spot the young cop who drove me over. I waved for him to join us.

"Who's that?" Hans asked.

"New uniform who wants to be a Homicide dick when he grows up."

Hans grunted.

"Officer Bartok," I began. "You know what 'lividity' is?"

"Uhh," he stammered. "When gravity causes blood and body fluids to go to the lowest extremities of a corpse?" It sounded like he memorized it right out of the textbook.

"Throw 'im a fish," Kemp said.

"Shut the fuck up, Dan," I put in. "He already sounds smarter than you."

Hans shot me a look.

"See anything unusual here, Bartok?" I prompted.

He stared at the body for several long seconds. His polished black shoes shuffled nervously in the sand. "No, sir."

"See the purple and red discoloration along the undersides of her legs, the back of the neck, and there on her back?"

"Yes, sir."

"That tell you anything?"

Bartok stared at the body, then shook his head.

"Remember where the lividity is — like she was laying on her back," I began. "Even though the body is, at present, positioned on its left side. Had the victim been killed where she is now, the lividity would have begun immediately—"

"— and the pooling of blood would appear along her left

side, not her back," Bartok finished.

Kemp sighed with exaggerated impatience.

"There's your first lesson in Homicide 101," I said. "You can take off now." Bartok nodded gravely and walked back past the yellow tape.

"Anyway," Hans said, "when the coroner's done, we'll roll her prints, run them through Cal-ID and see if we can get her a real name. Once we do, we'll need to get out to her place to see if there's more where she came from. In the meantime, I'll see how soon I can arrange for an autopsy."

For better or worse, the number of homicides perpetrated in L.A. dictated that personnel representing virtually every facet of police and related investigative work were on call seven days a week. Even so, it sometimes took days to get a victim on the table.

"Not that it hasn't been fun coming over to see you and all, Hans, but what am I doing here?"

My old partner glanced back toward the body. "Cuts on the hands, just like the others."

"Sonofabitch. I should have guessed."

"Sorry, Mike. We can use you on this."

"Anyone canvassed the immediate neighborhood yet? Maybe checked for surveillance videos that might have picked up the dump?" I asked.

"Not yet. Kemp, why don't you get going on that.... I'll have a uniform take the prints to the ID tech after you collect 'em."

Turning to face me, Hans said, "We'll give the fingerprint tech a head start on the ID, then we can take it from there."

" 'We' who?"

"I need you here for your brain, your history, Mike. No one

has the background on this that you've got. You're the only one who's visited all the crime scenes."

When I had taken my retirement, the biggest case I had been working was an apparent serial-killer situation that had involved, among other things, some very strange wounds on the hands of the victims. Not normal defense wounds from a knife-wielding attacker. Something else.

"This isn't my thing anymore, Hans. I sail boats, scuba dive. I don't need this shit."

"Nobody needs this shit, Travis. Least of all that girl over there. Go ahead, leave, take what you've got in your head. But if you don't work this, there's gonna be more just like her."

The bark and cry of seagulls carried on the breeze, and I stared out at the horizon.

"What? A consulting gig?" I asked.

"Right. And we finish this fucker off."

Hans flipped his notebook closed, then turned to see the coroner investigator stand and approach us.

"You want to take a look now? We're done with that part," the investigator said, referring to their photography exercise.

"Yeah, thanks," Hans said.

Hans and Kemp had arrived on the scene several minutes before either the coroner's investigator or the criminalist. What Hans had seen was enough for him to have called me.

Yamaguchi, Kemp and I turned back to the body, where I got a close-up look at the newest of my killer's victims.

She was blond and fit, maybe eighteen or twenty. She wore little makeup, and looked like she would have been an outdoors type, very likely a college student. The body was lying on its left side, its head partially resting on an outstretched left arm. The knees were loosely pressed together, slightly curled into a fetal position, as if she had simply chosen to lie down and gaze at the blue, rolling California surf.

Her milky green eyes reflected the morning sun in a way that seemed to amplify the timelessness of the unceasingly pounding waves, and the frailty of mortal existence. I searched her face and wished, as I often did, that I could read the last moments captured by those eyes, those still dying cells that held the face of a killer.

"Not much blood," Kemp said.

Not much. Only a fist-sized circle of dark brown on her beige cotton blouse, directly over her heart. I looked at the cuts. They were located on the webbing between her left thumb and forefinger, with several long, deep slices across the palm of that same hand. The right hand bore no cuts or wounds of any kind.

"No sign or evidence of resistance," I said. "Who's taking notes on the scene here?"

"I'm taking notes," Kemp said. "Sketches, too."

Hans nodded toward the coroner and crim. "Let's turn her over and see what we can find."

Carefully, they rolled her onto her back, and then on top of a black plastic sheet. Once on the plastic, the body could be shifted away and the area beneath it examined. I watched intently. Sometimes, particularly in serial situations, critical evidence is found in this manner, placed there intentionally by the killer. Serials often wanted to flaunt their prowess by taunting police. Superiority complexes were common among them.

This, however, had not been the case with the prior victims. Instead, the murderer had been more creative in his communications.

The imprint of the victim's body was barely perceptible in

the sand. Dan, Hans and I all balanced on our haunches, scrutinizing the area, our eyes squinting.

"Not even any blood on the sand," Kemp said aloud as he scratched out his notes.

"Nope," Hans said. "She was definitely killed elsewhere. Let's get the detectors and sifters going over here."

Hans stood and gave a very loud whistle to override the metal detectors' earphones. Looking up from his work, the nearest of the officers headed in our direction.

Moments later, the circular head of the detector was methodically passing over the area previously occupied by the young victim. I craned my neck for a look at the gauge on the handle of the device, hoping to see the needle spike on something. Something that could help identify the killer. A killer whose work I had taken into my dreams for the final two and one-half years of my career.

After several minutes, the officer shook his head at Hans.

"Shit," he muttered.

Now they would need to go through the same process with the sifters, a much more time-consuming process.

Kemp rose and headed-off toward the growing throng of onlookers, presumably to begin the task of interviewing the neighboring businesses and residents.

I turned to Jane Doe and the normally comforting sounds of the blue-green waves breaking against the sand. A beautiful set of three parallel swells moved toward the shoreline, preparing to carry a dozen or more wetsuit-clad surfers toward the beach that, for them, was a repository for surfboards and tanned bodies. They were blissfully oblivious to the death that had fouled it this morning.

I spent another long moment watching the surfers. I remembered those waves, riding them in, walking the board, splitting the world above from the one below. All just a pinpoint in time that will never come again, riding, riding....

The simplicity of those moments that I was sure would last forever, never to be trapped by a nine-to-five existence. I would fear no evil, no foul intrusions on free-form dreams as I curled forward, riding, riding...

But there I was in the real world. *Kehau* would get me out, though; a clean break on a broad reach, slicing the sea. The booming of a spinnaker filling —

"Bitch probably wouldn't give it up and the guy wasted her," Kemp said. "Cut-and-dried. She looks like the tease type."

Without thinking, I strode to where Kemp was talking with one of the patrol officers and a civilian with the unmistakable look of a print journalist, offering a batch of glib observations destined to be credited to "unnamed sources close to the investigation."

I grabbed a fistful of Kemp's clothing, the back of his shirt and the collar of his blue polyester sports coat, and pulled hard. Hard enough to knock him on his ass in the sand, where he landed with an *uumph* sound.

By the time he registered what had happened, I was in his face close enough to smell his cinnamon gum.

"Listen fuckhead," I said, my teeth clenched. "Keep your *opinions* to yourself. As soon as I decide whether to finish kicking your ass right here, I'm going to see if Hans can get you a well-deserved transfer to the Fraud unit. Until then, stuff a sock in it, and stay the hell out of my way."

The exchange was over before the media could record any of it, but not before Hans had come up beside me, taken hold of my elbow, and pulled me away from Kemp.

"God dammit, Travis! You're an *invited guest* on this trip..." He turned and pointed a stiff index finger at the stunned detective still seated in the sand. "And you, Kemp: save the colorful dialogue for your memoirs. Now get off your ass and get back to work."

Kemp's face was congested with surprise, humiliation, and anger.

I caught up with Hans a few paces later. I knew him well, and I could tell he was fighting off encroaching laughter.

"You shouldn't have done it, Mike, but I'm glad someone did. What a little prick." He paused, then added, "He's gonna write this up, you know."

"Fuck him," I said.

I turned around just as the body was being zipped into the black plastic bag. Two attendants carried it to a gurney waiting on the sidewalk just outside the yellow tape.

"So whattaya say, Mike?" Hans asked. "Sunset sailboat rides, or back to this shit?"

I hesitated. The sound of the surf filled my ears again.

"Get me back to Catalina, Hans. I've got to get some things in order over there. I'll let you know, okay?"

"You'll 'let me know'."

"Right."

"You know, Travis, you can be a bit of a prick yourself."

"Don't even start, Hans —"

He squinted his eyes into the glare on the horizon. "Do what you gotta do."

Chapter Three

THE FLIGHT BACK FROM THE MAINLAND SEEMED interminable. I should have felt relief putting distance between Jane Doe and Avalon, but Hans' words nagged at me, pissed me off. What right did he have to put the guilt on me? I did my twenty, and did them damn well. Hans more than anybody knew that. I was ten-seven. Out of service. Where I had chosen to be.

Images from the case files. Seven killings. Snippets of poetry hidden on the bodies. No connection among the victims. No pattern to the timing or the sequence of the murders. No sense to be made as to where the bodies had been found. Except they had all been dumped. and the cuts on the hands. Now Jane made eight.

The only way to solve a case like this was to get as far into the killer's head as you could and try to reach his next victim before he did. Then hope you could crawl back out again. It was an all-or-nothing choice, no middle ground.

I closed my eyes and let the rhythm of the pulsing rotor blades lull me into an uneasy sleep.

*   *   *

I WAS sitting alone in the late afternoon heat. Palm trees played shadows across white sand; my face upturned toward the sun. The whispering of the fronds sounded like falling rain, some hypnotic counterpoint to the ocean just a few yards away.

Then something else.

I listened.

A scream.

Another, this time piercing, surprised, frightened.

My eyes shot open. I was bare footed. I ran toward the scream, the sand burning, my legs pumping hard.

I crashed through a thatch of green bushes, my arms swinging wildly. Ferns and red ti plants and blood-red ginger broke and fell underfoot. I was winded.

Smash through, smash through.

There!

Another scream, close, so close.

I broke through onto a wide stretch of volcanic sand. I stood, my lungs heaving.

A calm, enclosed bay with deep blue water stretched out before me, shallow tidepools dotting the black shore.

Surreal.

I sucked at the thick, humid air. Sweat soaked my shirt clear through.

Something was in the pool nearest me. I ran toward it, and what I saw shut me down, caved my being, leaving me bloodless and terrified.

In the tidepool, face down, was my mother.

A running man receded into the shimmering heat. I brought up my Beretta in both hands, a perfect Weaver stance, and squeezed off four rounds, two-tapping the big automatic.

The bullets came out one by one, in slow motion, on jellied air, then dropped harmlessly to the black sand.

The distant figure stopped abruptly, turned to face me, and laughed.

*　　　*　　　*

I WAS awakened by the abruptness of the helicopter's landing, perspiring and with my heart racing. I glanced over at the pilot, but he was preoccupied. I sat for a long moment, then unbuckled my harness and climbed from the cockpit. What a fucking morning.

I rode back toward the harbor on my motorcycle, reliving The Dream in my mind. I had had it for years, certain details varying as I grew older, frames of reference changing, but essentially the story line remained the same. It captured well the discovery of my mother's body in a shallow swimming area near Puuhonua 'O Honaunau — The Place of Refuge. It's on the southwest coast of the big island of Hawaii, and is famous for spectacular snorkeling and diving. It's also the site of an ancient seaside citadel where common people could find asylum for breaking tribal *kapu*. The punishment was death.

I was thirteen at the time. My family had been spending some time at our home there, where we would often spend holidays and vacations. My mother was half Hawaiian, born and raised in the islands, and my father loved to take my brother and me there to learn about that part of our blood heritage. I would later share my mixed ancestry, both the prejudices and benefits, with a man in whom I would entrust my own life. My partner, Hans Yamaguchi.

My mother had been an excellent swimmer, practically born in the water, and frequently spent time alone with her thoughts in the silence of the clear depths of the bay, among the colorful tropical fish inhabiting that ancient place.

On a day she had been doing exactly that, I discovered her body floating about fifteen feet from shore. Before the tourists came, with their sunscreen and Frisbees. There at the water's edge. On that muggy, overcast morning I found my mother.

I will never forget how cold I was. My knees gave way. I was on the sand, kneeling, yelling at the top of my lungs.

When the police and ambulance arrived, I watched them place my mother on a stretcher, cover her head and face with the litter's white sheet, and load her body into the back of the red and white vehicle. My brother stood beside me, affording me whatever comfort a fifteen-year-old can to his younger sibling. Both of us stifled our tears. Father was busy with the police and ambulance crews. Shock forever preserved the tableau. I can summon it any time. The gray sky, my father moving among the uniformed men, flashing lights....

I couldn't bring myself to look at her at the funeral several days later, so that was the last I ever saw of her. A lifeless shape on a gurney, under a thin white shroud.

My father was never satisfied that it was a swimming accident. I wasn't either. But he would share his grief with no one, and bore it silently, plunging deeper and deeper into his work. Until he, too, finally died.

*　　*　　*

I WAS BACK aboard the *Kehau* by ten o'clock. Art was pac-
ing the dock that fronted the Harbor Patrol office, agitated.
When he saw me, he got into his Mako and beelined it over.

"Your charter came back about an hour ago," he said. "Rex
just left."

"So where'd they go off to?"

"Said they were canceling the rest of their charter with you.
Want their money back. I tried to talk them out of it, but —"

"Fuck it, Art, don't worry about it. I've got other things to
worry about anyway."

"Yeah, well... The daughter, whatshername?"

"Tiffany."

"Yeah, right. Tiffany. She wanted to tell you goodbye and
thanks. Rex said she seemed kind of embarrassed that her dad
was being such an asshole."

"Thanks again, Art."

If that was her dad's reaction to a few hours' unscheduled
absence, I could only guess how he'd feel about my sleeping
with his daughter.

My head was pounding, so I did the only thing that seemed
to make sense. I decided to go to Pete's Roadhouse, my
favorite Avalon bar.

I waited until eleven o'clock, trying to keep myself occupied checking the boat's engine, polishing brightwork, servic-
ing the scuba gear, and generally waiting for a respectable hour
to appear at the tavern. I decided that eleven o'clock was good
enough. Pete's didn't open until eleven.

By the time I had tied my skiff off at the pier and walked to
the Roadhouse's well-used — some would say battered — front
door, most of the usual coterie of regulars already had their

asses firmly planted in their usual positions. Heads turned reflexively to see who was dumping sunlight into their sanctuary. As the door swung shut, I was transformed from a faceless silhouette into Mike Travis, fellow traveler.

"Hey, Mike," came a bunch of voices. A ragged salutation. Maybe I went there too often.

Sometimes it just feels good to know you can count on certain things to remain unchanging, predictable. That's what I was looking for. Benign monotony. Something familiar, safe.

I casually waved at some die-hard locals, but headed over to the long bar which occupied an entire wall. A smoky mirror ran its length. Rows of ornate handles sprouted from the countertop and dispensed the finest collection of draft beers in Los Angeles County.

On the far end of the bar was a cash register, in front of which stood the owner, Pete, an unlit cigar clenched between his teeth. As always.

The air smelled of smoke, beer, and food from the kitchen that supplied Roadhouse patrons with some of biggest, greasiest, gut-busting hamburgers anywhere. The Stones' *Ruby Tuesday* was playing on the jukebox near the front door, and an animated game of pool was under way.

Pete's Roadhouse is not a large place by any means. It probably legally, seats about fifty or so, but I had seen it much more crowded than that.

I walked over to Pete and gave him a hearty handshake.

"Hey, Boss," I said. My usual greeting.

"How's it going, Mikey," he mumbled around the ever-present cigar. "I thought you left this morning."

News travels fast.

"No. Just flew over to L.A. for a few hours. My ex-partner

called me over on a case."

"Thought you were retired," he grunted.

"So did I."

"Well, you missed a good one last night." He laughed, the cigar rolling around between his teeth. "The Singin' Dude gets up and starts doin' a strip-tease just before last call. Just stands up and starts takin' it all off, man. Right up there on the bar, man, *on* the fucking bar!" He shook his head. "God it was funny. I guess the music got to him or something. Drunk as hell. I mean, man, if he didn't live in walking distance, I would have eighty-sixed his ass a lot earlier. Then these two tourist chicks stand up and join him. No shit, they *join* in! I just ran for the front door and locked it, so's no one would come in and bust us all.

"Anyway, they're all down to their skivvies, and I call it off. I mean, they weren't going to stop. God, it was funny, though. Ponytail Mike is right there eggin' 'em on, of course. I'm bettin' Singin' Dude is plenty hung over today."

"Maybe he took the two chicks home," I said.

"No fuckin' way."

There are three Roadhouse regulars named Mike. There's the quasi golf pro, Ponytail Mike, who sports a long black ponytail, as the name suggests; then there's Singin' Dude Mike, who is an electrical contractor on the island and has a penchant for singing *a capella* whenever the mood strikes and the jukebox is not otherwise engaged; and then there's me. I'm just plain "Mike." Sometimes "Mikey."

"How about an Asahi with ice?" I said, watching Pete. The ice was a habit I had picked up traveling in the tropics. You can't get a beer too cold.

"Go ahead and sit down and I'll have Deana bring it over."

He was still laughing at his own story.

"You're the man."

I wandered over to a table occupied by Ponytail Mike, who never seemed to actually golf despite his reputed profession; a local boat captain named Dave, whose nickname was "Yosemite Sam", because of his large drooping mustache and gravelly voice; and my buddy Rex, a former Navy SEAL, who was generally considered to be Avalon's finest boat-engine mechanic, and dive-boat skipper. Dave had taken Tiffany's parents on their impromptu fishing expedition. That these guys were already here explained how Pete knew I'd been gone.

I pulled out a stool and sat down.

"Big night last night, huh Ponytail?" I said. All three broke out in spontaneous laughter.

"Hell yes. Unreal, man. I have no idea what got into the Singin' Dude, but he sure put on a show. Shoulda let those two tourist chicks finish their act."

My beer was delivered moments later by a stunning brunette with unusually blue eyes, shapely legs, smooth skin, and a tan that belied her indoor line of work. Her thick hair was brushed straight back from her forehead and it hung just past her shoulders. It was generally believed she was in her mid-twenties. No one that I know had ever asked.

I had admired Deana, as had every other heterosexual male who met her, ever since she had started working at the bar. We all told Pete she was the best insurance that he could have against us drinking elsewhere. All he had to worry about was her opening her own place.

"Hey, Mikey," she said. She had a slightly crooked front tooth that gave her a sexy smile. She placed my beer and frosty glass of ice in front of me. "These guys tell you about the big show?"

"Sure enough," I answered, smiling, "I'm sorry I missed it."

"You didn't miss much." She paused momentarily, then added, "Now, if *you* had been dancing, that would have been something to watch." She winked and walked back toward the bar.

The table went silent.

"Well shit, Mike, that was a buy sign if I ever saw one," Dave said, incredulous.

"You got some beer foam in your mustache, Yosemite," I said, dismissing it.

My stock among my peers had just reached an all-time high. But it was true that despite the open display of admiration and lust among the patrons, Deana had somehow walked that razor-thin line between her professional life and her personal life. No one really knew who, if anyone, she dated. Which was doubly remarkable considering how small a town Avalon is.

I took a sip of beer, but couldn't taste it. Music and conversation echoed against my ears, but nothing got through. Only the sounds of breaking waves and seagulls, dead young women with eyes that held eternity. Blood on the sand. Blood on my hands. Hans.

"Hey, Mike... you with us, man?" I heard Rex say.

I blinked.

"You okay?" he asked.

"Yeah, I'm all right. I just had a couple of things blind-side me, that's all."

"The charter canceling?" Rex asked.

"I don't care about that."

"Then what's up, man?" Dave said.

"I got called back to consult on a murder case that looks like the same M.O. as one I was working just before I retired. A real ball-buster. I never really got to put it to bed, you know? It's nagged at me ever since. Unfinished business."

"So...? Out with it, bro," Rex said. "It'll probably do you good to talk about it anyway."

Everyone loves a cop story. So I filled them in on the grisly series of murders I had once investigated, and now found myself being drawn into again.

"About three years ago I got a call-out on a female body that had been found behind the Chateau Marmont — an old hotel in west L.A. —"

"That's where Belushi died, isn't it?" Ponytail Mike asked.

"Yeah. It was crawling with rock stars and actors in its day. The place is a little worse for wear now, though."

Yosemite gave Ponytail an impatient glance. "Stop interruptin'. You're always interruptin'."

I swallowed a slug of beer and wiped my mouth with the back of my hand. "Anyway, the victim had been killed somewhere else and dumped there. You could tell because there wasn't much blood at the scene. Turns out that she was a call girl. What was unusual about it, though, was that we found this weird sort of drawing under the body. It had been put there intentionally. The image was abstract and we couldn't figure it out, but the fact that it was there at all made it unusual."

I traced imaginary lines across the palm of my left hand. "There were several deep cuts on one of her hands."

Rex leaned toward me, intrigued. "What, like she had fought the guy off?"

"That's what I thought at first. But the cuts appeared on only one hand. Defense wounds would have been on both hands. And there wasn't really any sign that the victim had struggled.

No abrasions, bruises, that kind of thing. But I didn't have any better explanation for them, so I made note of it and moved on."

"So how was she killed?" Rex asked.

"Single stab wound to the heart."

"Quick and silent," Rex nodded knowingly, "SEAL training."

Bright daylight sliced through the room as two people entered the bar. The couple sauntered up to a pair of swivel stools at the bar, but the door remained open. Ponytail cupped a hand to his mouth and hollered, "Shut the door for Chrissakes." He shook his head in disgust and muttered something about fucking tourists.

"About six months later, I got a call on another body they found out at the Hollywood Bowl. Same M.O., single stab wound to the heart, deep cuts on the left hand. This one was a stripper."

Yosemite pulled at his mustache. "A call girl and a stripper."

"High-risk occupations," I agreed. "We found some weird artwork on that one, too. Another bizarre image that looked like reptile scales. That's when I knew we were in deep shit."

"Because of the pictures?"

"Yeah, but there's more to it. One killing is just a murder. Two is a series. I figured if there were two, there could be more. The only good news was that the killer had a definable signature."

Ponytail squinted. "What's a signature? He didn't like sign something left on the bodies, did he?"

Yosemite looked at him again, shook his head in disgust. "Jesus."

"No," I answered. "You know what an M.O. is, right?"

"Modus operandi," Ponytail said.

"Right. That's the 'how' of a killing. What kind of tools does the killer use, gun or knife, that sort of thing. The signature is more like the 'why' of it. It's a behavioral clue. You begin to understand their psyche, their motivation. It's what makes him unique."

"So what'd you do?"

"Long story short, I ran the details through the FBI's VICAP computer files and got five more hits in other states."

"Holy shit." Yosemite said.

And on it went, for another three or four rounds of drinks, each of us taking our turn paying Deana.

When I had finally finished and brought the story current, Ponytail consulted his Rolex, let a respectable period of silence pass, then announced that he had to go. Dave and Rex took their turn at the pool table.

I felt better having had the opportunity to vent somewhat. Nothing too deep. No demons. No dreams.

I looked at my watch, and determined that I had been at Pete's for three hours, and determined further that I had, somewhere along the way, acquired a not-insignificant buzz. Music and smoke continued to fill the dark, nautically decorated bar. I tapped my fingers on the table absently as I listened to the jukebox and watched my friends play pool.

Sensing a presence close behind me, I looked to my right, but saw only Deana's long, slender fingers coming to rest on my shoulder. She had her arm around me, a bemused look on her face.

She put her cocktail tray down on my table. "Want to talk about it?"

"Talk about what?" I said.

She shrugged. "You look lost."

I didn't answer.

"Could be good for both of us, Mike."

"Why? You lost, too?"

Picking her tray up off the table, she began to move away.

"Wait," I said abruptly. "What time are you off?"

Deana arched an eyebrow. Waited a few beats.

"Seven."

I must have had more to drink than I thought, because I had just broken Mike Travis' Cardinal Rule. Don't date where you drink. It's a hell of alot easier to find a good date than to find a good bar.

Chapter Four

THE ANACONDA CLUB DIDN'T GET CRANKING until well after ten. He liked to arrive early, though, and get the booth in the corner near the long bar. He could see everything from there, practically the entire dance floor, the DJ booth, and most importantly, he could see everyone who came in the door.

He liked this hour of the evening. This was when the secretary types came in, taking a walk on the wilder side of the Strip. They'd trade their conservative business suits for tight fitting slut-wear, drink a little too much, maybe do a couple lines, an amyl popper, and lose themselves in the throb of sweat and smoke and sex.

Twin ropes of blue-gray cigarette smoke poured from his nostrils as he swirled his glass. He lifted it to his nose and inhaled the leathery odor of Jack Daniel's, then brought it to his lips and emptied it with one quick flick of his wrist. It was hot going down, and he felt a surge of excitement. *Oh, yeah.* He was beginning to come on to the acid.

The waitress returned with another double JD and he asked for a couple of extra napkins. When she walked away he pulled a pen from his black leather jacket and began to draw. It was always like this. First shapes and strange symbols, then the words would come. Stimulating, beautiful words. Some people thought they were sick, the things he wrote. But they didn't understand. They didn't *know*.

A trio of young women took their place at the bar. The one in the blue was looking at him. She smiled. The other two looked over, whispered something to the one in blue, then looked away

He liked to watch people, particularly women, and tried to find their secret weakness. Everyone had a hole to fill, didn't they? A secret desire, or a vulnerability to be exploited? They were so predictable, really.

The women at the bar were talking. Animated gestures. Smiles split painted faces. He knew the show was for him.

He sat content in his dark corner, allowing the chemicals inside him to work their magic while he wrote on the white paper napkins. Now and then he would glance over toward the bar and catch the woman in blue looking at him. When she saw him, she quickly looked away.

She wasn't pretty, really. But not unattractive either. Just plain. Yes, that was it. Plain. It was the ones you wouldn't ordinarily notice that you had to keep your eye on.

Her dark hair was pulled back from her face and into a tight knot at the back of her head. Shiny earrings that were much too long wriggled and glinted in scattered light as she moved. Her body language told him she was not close friends with the two women she sat with, and that was the way he liked it. It helped that she was the fifth wheel, the homely friend that the pretty ones brought along to preen and strut in front of.

It was the unbeautiful ones that you wanted, though. They weren't used to being approached by handsome men in bars, and were so receptive to the promise of romance. This was how you separated the weak ones from the herd. They were so willing and eager. So trusting of a stranger, while the pretty ones were too difficult and unmanageable.

The blonde in red shot him a prick-teasing glance that he ignored, focusing his attention instead on the women in the blue dress. He gave her a smile and she looked down shyly. The red dress noticed and turned her back to him, blocking his view of the plain one in blue. That was good. A little competition made things that much easier for him.

He would take his time, though, and make his approach slowly. This was not something to be rushed. Quite the opposite. It was to be savored, relished.

The night was young. There was time. Plenty of time. There would be lots and lots of time.

*　　　*　　　*

"MAENADS," the old woman said to the small gathering. Her voice sounded dusty and hoarse. "Hear me now, for it is time."

His mother stood with the others in solemn silence.

"Cybele, Great Mother, accept our sacrifice in honor of the Twice Born."

He stood alone beside the old woman, the flickering of yellow candle-light making deep shadows dance along the walls. The animal squirmed in his hands and he stroked and tried to calm it.

"Semele, burned by the immortals," she chanted.

The boy responded as he had been taught. "Semele, retrieved from the Underworld and resurrected as Thyone."

"Semele, mother of the Twin."

"The Twin who is good and kind to those who honor him. The Twin who brings madness and destruction to those who displease him." The animal wriggled as he spoke, desperate to be let go. The boy squeezed it gently.

The group took up the last of the incantation. "The Twin whose blood runs among us."

"In any generation..." the old woman intoned.

"...there can be only one," the assembly concluded in unison.

His mother stepped forward and reached for the kitten the boy held. His stomach clenched as he momentarily thought of resisting. She took it, then walked slowly to the table beside him. It squealed pitifully as she turned the tiny animal on its back and held it there. The old woman withdrew a shiny blade and offered it to the boy. The mewling grew louder in his ears, and he couldn't avoid seeing the animal's terrified eyes as he approached.

Its tiny head whipped from side to side, unable to escape.

The blade followed its sanctified journey. Blood seeped down to the floor and onto the boy's bare feet.

Chapter Five

IWALKED THE MILE OR SO THROUGH THE BUSY summertime streets of Avalon, back down to the pier where I had tied my skiff, the *Chingadera*. I call it a skiff, but it is actually a seventeen foot Boston Whaler. Overpowered with an Evinrude 90 outboard engine and center steering console, it is great as both a shore boat and a dive boat. Not bad for water skiing either. The walk did wonders sweating-out the effects of the last few hours of beer and conversation.

I sorted through my options with Deana and settled on dinner at my family's old house on the hill. It overlooks the harbor and has a picture-postcard view of the old Casino. I needed to call the caretakers as soon as I got back aboard the *Kehau* so the could get things organized. That would allow them just enough time to prepare the menu I had in mind, and get things shipshape while I collected my messages and got cleaned up.

Pulling alongside the *Kehau*, I tied the Whaler off so that it wouldn't scar the larger boat's pristine white hull, and climbed aboard. It was a rare day that I didn't register raw pride in my yacht.

The workmanship was outstanding. Below decks, I had personally designed the salon. It boasted a state-of-the-art satellite navigation and communications area that was positioned so that I could easily get above and below in the event I was sailing alone. In addition, I had a top-of-the-line laptop computer. I could send and receive email and faxes via satellite telephone, as well as catalog my thoughts and ideas. It also handled my former case notes.

The remainder of the salon was set up as a living room and dining room, complete with built-in surround audio, television, and a wet bar with ice maker. The galley occupied the space just forward of the living and dining area. Portholes both starboard and port allowed abundant natural light when the curtains weren't closed. The living quarters, consisting of four separate staterooms, were down another short set of stairs immediately forward of the galley.

I felt her rock gently in the wake of a passing vessel as I climbed the stairs to the enclosed wheelhouse above. It reminded me how tender she could be in a beam sea. I wiped a handprint from the bulkhead before reaching for the chart that sat on the nav table. My plans for a trans-pacific trip to Kona got folded away along with the map, and I placed it among the others in the drawer beside the GPS.

I spent another few moments idly organizing the wheelhouse, placing my dive and equipment maintenance logs in their proper places. After kicking off my sandals, I descended the stairs and went to the laptop to check my e-mail. There was none. It felt more like an end than a beginning.

*   *   *

STANDING beneath the massaging spray of hot water in the master head's spacious shower stall, I closed my eyes, and absorbed its muscle-relaxing oscillation. Blood, sand and violent death again invaded the darkness behind my eyes. Then the weight of Hans' words heaved against what remained of the serenity I had been so slowly regaining at the helm of the *Kehau*.

My mind methodically reviewed the ugly scene at Venice Beach, and I finally began to come to terms with my decision. I weighed the cost of the peace I was about to give up against the need to finish what the killer had started. The answer came clear. My best thinking always seemed to take place in the shower.

Regardless of the personal price, I was needed back on the mainland. The darkness was pulling me back, but this time the son of a bitch was going to pay.

I dressed in khaki shorts and a dark blue Hawaiian-print shirt for my dinner with Deana. Standing at the *Chingadera*'s console, I glided across the harbor's smooth emerald surface toward the pier, breathing deeply the calm summer air. Waning sunlight blinked against storefront windows and I thought again of my return to L.A. The calm before the storm.

*   *   *

I SLID the Yamaha into a vacant spot immediately in front of Pete's Roadhouse. Lifting my Neptune sunglasses to perch on top of my head, I sat astride the bike and waited for Deana.

Deana opened the door. She was wearing a short black skirt

and low-cut white tee shirt. A leather backpack/purse was slung casually over her right shoulder.

She flashed a brilliant smile at me, her blue eyes holding mine.

I got off the bike and bowed.

"Welcome to the free world, ma'am" I said. "Rhett Butler."

"Why, Mistah Travis," she said, giving me Scarlett O'Hara. "Y'all realla do know haw to chahm a lady."

"How 'bout a ride to yo' plantation for a change of clothes?"

Delicate lines radiated from the corners of her eyes. "Mistah Travis, I thought you would nevah ask."

She climbed aboard and struck a natural balance, apparently no stranger to motorcycles. She leaned and balanced expertly with every turn until we got to her apartment building. It was vintage early 1930's, an echo of Avalon's hacienda heyday.

I pulled the bike into a space reserved for motorcycles. Deana waited for me to turn off the engine and set the kickstand.

"C'mon up, I'll get ready real quick, Then we can go, 'kay?" It was not really a question. "So, where are you taking me?" she added without a pause.

"A very exclusive place."

"C'mon, really. I need to know how to dress."

"Okay, it's my family's old home up the hill." I pointed in the general direction of the stately old house.

"Great! What do want me to wear?"

I smiled for what felt like the first time in hours. "Something comfortable."

The lobby of her building was decorated with ornate tile in a Spanish motif. Our footsteps echoed on the hard floor. We arrived at her front door, second floor above the main entrance.

Her front window was ajar about four inches.

"Did you leave that window like that?" I asked.

"I most shorely did, Mistah Travis."

"I'm serious."

"Sure. I leave it like that every day...especially when it's hot like this. Otherwise it's a sauna."

"You know, a person could reach right through this window and open your front door. Did you know that?" I demonstrated by doing exactly that.

"But it's just *Avalon*, Mike. I mean, like that's gonna happen?"

"You're asking the wrong guy, Deana."

"Gotcha," she said.

We entered her small apartment. Everything was nice and tidy. Paperback books and magazines, framed photos here and there. The pictures showed Deana in various poses, with different groups of people, some of whom I recognized from around Avalon. They were all quite recent.

The walls had floral lithographs by Laguna Beach artist, John Botz. Pillows on the couch picked up colors from the artwork. Several vases, both fresh and silk flowers.

I'd lost count of how many apartments I had entered as a cop. Burglary, domestic violence, and worse. The ugliness was somehow magnified when it happened in places like Deana's. Where the scent of candles and potpourri mingled with the sweat and cigarettes of crime scene investigators.

"So, make yourself comfortable. I'll be done in just a couple minutes."

I sat back on the sofa, and picked up a *People* magazine. This issue had some new young movie starlet I couldn't identify on the cover, looking tattooed and greasy. Flavor-of-the-month face staring out from glossy pages. Before long the smugness of youth would erode into deep lines of fast living, drugs and turmoil. The road goes on forever, and the party never ends. Sure.

I heard the shower turn off, and the sounds of closet-rummaging. Minutes later, Deana reappeared in the living room wearing a pair of khaki shorts, sandals, and a sleeveless white blouse, tied in a knot just below her breasts, revealing a lovely brown midriff. A simple gold chain necklace draped her throat.

"Am I okay?" she asked.

"Well beyond 'okay'."

Her gaze was honest, open. "Good," she said.

"Ready to go then?"

"Ready."

Deana left one light glowing dimly from her bedroom. She lit another beside the sofa, then crossed to the small window beside the front door and made a show of closing and latching it.

Again, her look was direct. "Thanks for caring, Mike."

I closed the door behind us and tested the handle. I started up the bike and took her the long way up on the winding roads to the house. Warm fingers of wind stroked our faces while vapor trails cut tinted patterns across a magenta sky.

*   *   *

WE PULLED up onto the aged brick driveway, lined on either side with graceful queen palms, each individually lit from powerful, recessed spotlights near the bases of the thirty- foot trees. Thick vines of bougainvillea crawled the tan stucco walls splashing red, pink and purple beside the Spanish-style door.

I killed the Yamaha's noisy engine and we were enveloped in exaggerated silence.

"Wow," Deana said. "This is *gorgeous*. How big is this place?"

"It's about three acres. There's also a small cottage over that way," I said, pointing down the slope.

"Unbelievable."

I punched a ten-digit code on the keypad mounted in the wall, then took a key from my pants pocket. I pushed the door open to reveal a generous entry, decorated mostly in heavy wooden antiques from Spain and Mexico. There was an expansive view from the oversized bay windows.

The caretakers, an older couple named Brooks, who had held the position for many years, had taken pains to light the house, and select some pleasant music. I recognized Antonio Jobim's romantic, Brazilian jazz playing on the stereo. Nice choice.

Deana walked slowly down the corridor leading to the living room. Along the walls hung numerous photographs of my father with various dignitaries, mixed-in with numerous covers of national business and news magazines, each individually illuminated by tiny pin spotlights recessed into the ceiling.

"Is this your father?" Deana pointed to one of the photos.

I nodded. "He was really something."

"Wow, look at these: *BusinessWeek, Fortune, Forbes, Inc.,* even *Time* and *Newsweek.* God, Mike!"

I remained silent.

"A picture with Kissinger and Nixon, for Christ sake..." she began reading the captions to the magazines' cover photos. "His name is Van de Groot? What's up with *that*? Yours is Travis, right?"

I smiled. That was not a story I told very often.

"It is *now,* anyway. Travis is really my middle name. My mom was half-Hawaiian, and my dad was Dutch. The name my parents gave me when I was born was 'Michael Travis Kamahale-Van de Groot.'"

Her eyebrows went up, a look often given to Pete's customers.

"You must have been teased to death as a kid," she said.

"Yeah, some. But Dad was pretty well known, so I was more in danger of concentrated ass-kissing than much real teasing. Even my school teachers would tiptoe around me."

"Poor little rich boy," she said, her expression robbing the words of sarcasm.

"Anyway, let's move past the gallery here, and into the living room," I said as I placed my hand at the small of her back, and gently nudged her. "I've got wine — red or white — cocktails, and cold beer. Any of those sound good? My turn to bring the drinks."

"That will be a pleasant change, Mr. Travis," she smiled. "I'll have red wine. What kind do you have?"

"Californian or French."

"Choose for me."

"My pleasure."

I turned and opened the small door that led to the wine cellar.

"I'll be right back," I said glancing over my shoulder to catch Deana's eye.

I returned from the wine cellar moments later with two bottles of French Pauillac, vintage 1977, lightly frosted with fine dust. I placed them on the counter top of a sunken bar.

Deana sat on a stool and watched me go through the motions of properly decanting a bottle of well-aged fine wine. This was one of the many skills taught me by my late father that I was never able to thank him for.

As I grew older, I found that there were many of these social skills I had good cause to be grateful for, but I had taken them for granted, even resented them, as a kid. Hard lessons.

But great for impressing women.

After decanting the wine into a lead crystal decanter, allowing the fine sediment to slowly find its way to the bottom of the cruse, I sniffed the cork, and tasted the wine. Rich, full bodied, and a hint of smoke. Perfect. I filled a bulbous, long stemmed cabernet glass about one-third full, and delivered it into Deana's smooth, sun-browned hand. For the briefest moment we touched.

"Thanks."

I poured a glass of the Pauillac for myself, then led the way to the French doors that opened onto the veranda. Avalon's lights twinkled below. We stood and admired the dying sunset.

Lights on the boats far below us probed the warm dusk of the evening. Jasmine mingled sensually with the salt breeze off the ocean.

Both of us got lost in our separate thoughts, until a boat's horn blared. Deana jumped, startled.

I laughed.

"I guess I was lost in the mood," she said, and laughed, too.

I stepped over to a hidden panel, turned a couple of knobs, and music from within the house was brought outdoors. Soft lighting washed the trunks of the potted palms that lined the patio wall and bathed the green fronds in warm light. Shadows cast by the swaying leaves created a rhythmic pattern on the walls. The breeze buffeted against us. The music enfolded us.

We watched the sky fade from purple to black.

*   *   *

WE SAT at the informal dining table and finished the last of our dinners of broiled *mahi-mahi,* jasmine rice with coconut milk, and a fresh green salad. As we emptied our second bottle of wine, Deana probed my background. It was not something I usually gave in to.

"So, tell me more about your family. I mean, I don't even know why your dad was on those magazine covers."

I pushed through my reticence and cleared my throat. "My father was the founder of what is now one of the two or three largest venture capital firms in the country. Among the top ten in the world, in fact: Van de Groot Capital, or VGC for short."

"I've heard of that, I think."

"You probably have. The firm has relationships with some of the wealthiest and most influential companies, not to mention individuals, all over the world." I picked up the bottle. "More?"

"Not yet, thanks. But go on," she said.

"The money that is entrusted to VGC by those investors is pooled together, then *re*-invested into other companies, usually in exchange for majority ownership of those companies."

I killed the Pauillac.

"Later, sometimes years later, those companies are 'taken public' by virtue of public stock offerings made through one of the stock exchanges in the U.S. or abroad —- you know, like the New York Stock Exchange or the NASDAQ. Anyway, when things work the way they are supposed to, VGCC's investors make many times their original investment, and everyone is very happy."

"So that's how your father got so famous? Picking companies to invest in?" Deana asked.

"That's pretty much it. Over the years, my father gained a reputation as a business guru, and a bit of a celebrity, too."

"So why aren't you the president of the company or something? Being a cop seems a long way off from Wall Street."

"It's complicated," I said, pushing my chair back.

"Sorry. If it's none of my business...but, I really want to know. I want to know about you," she persisted.

"Why?"

She hesitated.

"I've watched you. Like at Pete's, the way you sit so your back never faces the door. Or the way your eyes move, sizing people up. Not offensive, but always watching. Always ready for something."

I watched her search my face.

"Even when you laugh with your friends it seems like you're holding something back. There's so much — I don't know exactly — *caution* in you."

She shrugged, tilting her head in the candlelight. "I don't know, you're just... *different*."

"And that's good?"

Her sapphire eyes were direct. "I'd like to think so."

"What does that mean, exactly?"

Wax dripped down a tapered candle. "That I'm a little nervous around you. You're a dangerous man, Mike Travis."

I smiled. "But fairly tame with civilians."

"And bad guys?"

"Not so tame," I said. "Let's go outside."

Her hand was warm. Her cheeks flushed as she stood. We took our wine to the veranda and let the night drift up to us. I kissed her softly. She closed her eyes and returned it with a passion and a sweetness that surprised me. We let the moment linger.

"So tell me, Mike," she whispered.

Somehow, telling her seemed natural.

"All right. Here it is: ever since I was old enough to recognize it, maybe eleven years old or so, I saw that the Van de Groot name opened all kinds of doors.

"Because the company was so successful," I said, gesturing toward the hallway where the framed magazine covers and photos were hung. "And the firm was so well known, people would often go to great lengths to ingratiate themselves with my father. His *influence* I mean, not really my *father* personally. Well, that started to happen to me, too. I would be given special privileges and things, even as a kid, that I knew were only because of my dad."

"Some people really get off on that kind of favoritism," Deana said.

"Well, I had the opposite reaction. I always went the extra mile to win contests, get grades — and girls — on my own. Not just because I was the son of a wealthy and famous man.

"Needless to say, mine is a pretty unique name, what with 'Kamahale-Van de Groot' and all. So when the time came to apply to college, I did it without using my last name. I wanted to get in on my own merit."

"They must have been proud of you for that," Deana said.

I shook my head.

"My dad about disowned me when he found out, and I guess I don't blame him now that I'm older. But I hadn't intended any disrespect. I'd like to believe, ultimately, that he understood."

She looked away.

"So, after college, why didn't you go back to your real name? And what about the company?"

"When I turned nineteen, I changed my name *legally*; by dropping *both* of my last names. By that time, I had decided I was going into law enforcement, and I really didn't want my father's political influence to affect my career. I wanted to be a cop, and a good one. On my own."

"What did your dad do?"

"He was furious. Really thought it was disgraceful and disrespectful to both sides of the family. It's ironic, because my intentions had been exactly the opposite. I wanted to succeed, and make my family proud, but not on the coattails of our family name. I was naive and thought they would appreciate my determination."

"And they didn't?"

"In the end, most of them were understanding. Some never got over it. Anyway, by that time, my older brother had pretty much declared himself a VGC man, and joined the ranks about a year later when he earned his degree. He ended up taking over the presidency when my father died."

"Any regrets?" she asked.

"No. I threw my energy into being a cop. Now I devote my energy to my charter business, and beautiful young women who listen to me talk," I finished with a smile.

We leaned against the railing and the breeze ruffled her hair. "What about your mom? What was she like?" She spoke softly.

The breeze scurled around my heart, slowing it.

"Mike...?"

"Sorry," I said.

"I didn't mean to pry —"

"It's okay."

She watched the lights in the harbor below.

"Fact is, it was a long time ago."

"But it hasn't healed." A statement.

"No. It hasn't healed. Nightmares, that sort of thing. One dream, mostly, repeating itself over and over."

She didn't look at me and I loved her for that. It came easy, telling her. Like I was in a confessional. I let it out. The running. The hot sand. My mother's body in the pooling water. My useless gun and the laughing man....

"Could you see his face?" she asked.

"What?"

"The man in your dream, running away. Could you see his face?"

"No." A shiver ran through me. "Anyway, that's enough about me. Let's talk about you."

One thing about being a cop, you can read the signs that someone is stressed. She held the stem of her wine glass between her fingers and twirled it.

"I don't have a lot to tell. I'm adopted, so there's a lot I don't know."

"Who adopted you? How old were you?" I prompted.

She searched my face again.

"About a week or two after I was born, I think. Can you imagine that," Deana said, turning to me with eyes that had gone suddenly hard. "I mean, actually having a baby, caring for it, and feeding it day after day, then...just...giving it away? That's cold."

I let the silence hang.

"Not only that, I didn't even *find out* I was adopted until my sixteenth birthday, when I went to the DMV to get my driver's license. I remember I was so excited to drive. My mom went to the window with me, carrying my birth certificate, and the guy at the window says something like, 'Just a minute, I'll be right back,' then goes and talks to some other guy at a desk a few feet away. It's like I see them talking to each other, the window guy pointing toward me, then they both look at me, then look away and keep talking. I was *so* embarrassed, I didn't know what was going on..."

The pain of playing it back seemed to numb her.

"Anyway," she continued, "To make a long story short, as they say, both of the guys come back to the window and ask my mother and me to step out of line and come talk to them.

"It turns out that the birth certificate is fake. We leave the DMV office, me feeling like some kind of *criminal*, and Mom's eyes all misty. She tells me she adopted me — less than completely officially — when I was just a baby. I was so fucking *stunned* I couldn't believe it."

Somewhere above in the cavern of stars, a plane droned along its journey.

"Well, I decided then and there, fuck this. I can't count on anyone to tell me the truth, and I made up my mind that when I turned eighteen, I would take off and start a life that was under *my* control.

"You know, at least when I would get burned under those circumstances, it would be *my* doing, not some goddamn *surprise*."

I nodded. "I can understand that."

"Sorry. It's still a pretty sore spot. Anyway..." her voice trailed off. "Where's your adoptive mom now?" I asked.

"You mean little Mary Woods?" she said with a sardonic tone. "She's still in Pomona where I grew up."

"Where do things stand between you and her?"

"Nowhere," she said firmly, finally.

"Did you ever find out who your birth parents are?"

"Look, Mike. You shared with me tonight. I respect that. I'm really glad you did. But this thing with me, I'm just not ready — "

"It's okay."

Then it burst inside her, that ruptured membrane that held back the hurt and anguish.

"Deana —" I pulled her against me.

"They gave me away, Mike." Her shoulders heaved. "First they nursed me. Then they gave me away. Just like that."

I held her close.

"Why should I want to know who *they* are. I'm here now. I'm building a life *here*."

I felt for her. I had trod similar territory myself, and it was dangerous. It carried the power to drag you down for good, whether you saw it coming or not. The lucky ones overcame their history, closed the circle, and got on with life. The rest were simply crushed under the weight.

"I'm sorry, Deana."

We stood beside the rail a while longer, miles apart, separated only by inches.

Chapter Six

FELICIA VANSON TOOK STOCK OF HER IMAGE IN his bathroom mirror, checking again for flaws in her make-up. The idea, of course, was to look as if she wasn't wearing any. Tonight she had won a chance to impress the dark and handsome man from the Anaconda. She had never seen her girlfriends so mad, and secretly reveled in knowing that she had bested them. She ought to thank them. If they hadn't left in such a huff, she wouldn't have had the opportunity to accept his invitation back to his place.

God, what a night!

Now, as she finished her primping, smoothing wrinkles from her blue dress, Felicia felt that tingle of excitement that her mother used to call "butterflies." She wanted to impress him, but her unremarkable face gazed back at her from the mirror. She looked much younger than her twenty-four years, but her appearance had lately become a source of self-conscious irritation. She wanted to look more *sophisticated*, more *mysterious,* like those dark-haired beauties with bee-sting lips that pouted from the covers of all the fashion magazines. She sighed nervously as she stashed her hairbrush back in her purse, popped a breath mint in her mouth, and closed the door behind her.

He was standing just outside the door. He had that engaging half-smile that Felicia had found so disarming on his manchild face. It struck her again that he could look at once so youthful, and yet so worldly.

A full head taller than she, he had a well muscled chest that tapered to narrow hips. Dark curly hair hung to his shoulders, framing his high cheekbones and strong, square jaw. She loved how his blue eyes contrasted with the olive tone of his skin. Mostly, though, she was taken by his *presence.*

His apartment was simple and looked like it belonged to a college student. Rows of paperback books on makeshift plywood shelves; a ratty-but-clean couch fronted by a secondhand coffee table; some odd-looking lamps; a stereo and about two dozen candles.

Small casement windows were covered by Venetian blinds, lowered against the night.

"I'm drinking wine. You?" He held up an inexpensive bottle of Chianti.

"Sure," Felicia answered, already feeling more comfortable, her nerves calming. "I like your place," she offered.

"Thanks," he said, "it's not really mine. A friend lets me stay here, and keep some of my books and stuff. More like a friend of a friend, really. Anyway, the guy's away for a while, so I guess it's mine for now."

Felicia wandered about the small space, perusing the titles

of the books on the shelves: textbooks and poetry for the most part.

He poured a glass of wine and walked toward her, motioning as he did to the couch that sat under a sixties-era concert poster announcing Big Brother and the Holding Company together with the Grateful Dead at the Fillmore West.

An awkward moment of silence passed before Felicia filled it with: "So what do you do for a living?"

She immediately regretted the banal question, cringing inwardly.

If the young man was bothered, he did not show it. That was what made him so unusual. Nothing seemed to change his countenance or alter his demeanor. He was perpetually locked into some intense other-space. He was so much more composed than she. Not so much a matter of behavior, more like an *aura* that surrounded him. At times, his blue eyes were seductive, half-lidded, peering into that other place.

Felicia felt on the defensive, as if she had to keep up with him. It wasn't a completely bad feeling. On the contrary, it was almost sexual. A challenge to maintain a place in his world, a world she wanted desperately to enter, lithe, desired, her ordinary face hot with a sensuous beauty.

"For a living? This and that," he shrugged dismissively. "How about you?" He hated this part.

"I'm an accountant. Boring, huh?"

"What do you like to do when you're not working?"

She felt a wave of self-consciousness. Her life was so *boring*. Ever since college it had been work, work and work. She liked to club-hop with friends sometimes, but other than that she just read books.

"Check out the clubs on the Strip," she answered.

He nodded.

"And I like to read," she concluded honestly. "You?"

"I've always been a reader, too," he answered with more directness than she had expected. "Poets, social outcasts and critics, especially. People like Rimbaud, Blake, Nietzche, Kafka, you know...." he trailed off.

"I saw some of those on the shelves..."

"Yeah. My friend reads alot of the same stuff. '60's poetry and philosophy. I'm drawn to that."

"I can't say I really know much about it. I've never read that sort of thing."

"There was such *intensity* in that time — the Sixties, I mean," he continued. "You know, people were smoking dope, dropping acid. A real edgy period, man." He stopped abruptly, catching himself.

"What?" Felicia asked, prompting him.

"I get carried away sometimes," he answered. It was almost an apology, but not quite. "I've gotta be honest with you. You caught my eye from the minute you came into the club tonight."

Felicia was surprised and flattered by his admission, but said nothing. Oddly, she sensed him grow somehow darker, withdrawn, just momentarily, but perceptibly.

"Most guys prefer my friends." She hesitated, fishing for affirmation.

"No, there's something special about you. Smart guys would know it. I bet some have," he said smoothly.

"A few," she lied. "So... show me around."

He reached out for Felicia's empty glass and carried it to the kitchen counter together with his own. He refilled them both and returned.

At last he broke the awkward silence.

"Not much to see, really. Like I said, most of this doesn't belong to me. What's mine is mostly books and CDs. The rest belongs to Bob — that's the guy whose place this is."

"Oh," Felicia sighed, feeling awkward. She was waiting for him to make some kind of move.

"I'll tell you what: How about you look around on your own. I've got something to take care of in the kitchen, okay?"

"Sure, great." Her voice was tinted with disappointment.

A small desk was situated adjacent to the bookshelves and held a laptop computer, a fairly elaborate compact color printer, desk lamp, and the assorted bric-a-brac that desks seem to collect. She browsed aimlessly, wandering down the hall to the two bedrooms, peeked in, then returned to the living room.

During the next thirty minutes, she surprised herself by consuming another two and a half glasses of wine and was feeling loose. Funny, but she did not mind the absence of conversation, as it only seemed to heighten her curiosity and attraction to her enigmatic host.

During her self-guided tour, he had moved from the kitchen only to change the music on the CD player to some unfamiliar rock music.

"The Doors," he volunteered, answering the curious look she wore.

He had lit a number of candles, leaving them as the only illumination in the small room. He motioned toward the sofa for her to sit again as he moved to join her.

The butterflies returned, and she thought that now was the moment she had been anticipating. She wanted his hands on her.

The combined effects of the candlelight, anticipation and wine were conspiring to make her feel so *different*. Sort of free and unburdened, but with an undertone of unease, even fear. Irrational feelings for sure, yet her host's demeanor had subtly changed. He had become more intense, even agitated, about something.

There was a different kind of light in his deep blue eyes.

"Like I said, Felicia, you're very attractive to mc. I was watching you from the first moment I saw you. Did you know that? You're very unique. Very *special*."

Felicia self-consciously pulled at the hem of her blue dress and laughed.

"I don't know what to say. I mean..."

He broke into her thoughts. "Have you ever been high?"

"You mean marijuana or something? No, not much," she abruptly replied. Felicia reached for her wine and took a sip. "It's not exactly what boring accountants do."

He raised his eyebrows in disbelief.

"Well, maybe a joint now and then," she added with an empty laugh.

"No, I mean *really* high, like acid. LSD. Mind-blowing, breakthrough kind of high."

"God, no," she answered too quickly, with a tingle of anxiety. Fclicia wanted so badly for him to accept her.

"It'll change your life, I guarantee it," he said with a beautiful smile.

He produced a small glassine envelope containing what looked like small slips of paper, each one smaller than a postage stamp.

Felicia's heart began to race. "Change my life?"

He smiled and glanced down at her wine glass. A stillness played between them.

"What?" She asked. There was something not entirely playful about all this anymore.

He said nothing, only held her with his eyes.

"*What?* You *dosed* me?" She felt like screaming.

"Just relax, Felicia. We'll turn up the music, talk a little. I'll even read to you. Then, we'll just wait. It'll be great, man."

Her throat closed around her words.

"See? I'll do it, too." He took a tiny bit of the paper and placed it on his tongue. The half-lidded eyes closed. A smile touched his mouth, more a tremor. Then he swallowed.

"*Relax?*" she seethed. "I can't be*lieve* you'd do this to me!"

His features hardened. "Don't take that tone with me, Felicia. I'm doing you a favor."

She tried to stand, to leave, but found she couldn't. Her legs wouldn't cooperate.

The music took on a swirling, carnival-like sonance, but somehow ominous, incongruous. It charged the air with foreboding, like the soundtrack to a surrealistic dream. Hysteria tore at her insides and she tried to subdue it.

He smiled patiently, lighting a fresh stick of incense. A ribbon of blue smoke rose in a double-helix, an unearthly strand of DNA.

"The acid's called 'windowpane,' and it should be kicking in any time now... Just try to stay calm, and open your mind. You'll start to hear your own thoughts as if you're speaking them." His voice possessed an almost hypnotic quality as he spoke to her.

"Before long," he continued, "it'll seem like you can even *see* the music. Colors will be brighter, sounds will be more intense."

She felt the first wave of the drug wash over her. Against her will, Felicia became enthralled with the incense that twined around itself, pulsing, twisting on ethereal currents, finally floating free about the table.

Felicia stared at the floor, hysteria sluggish now, a hollow fear, as a black abyss fell away beneath the small couch. She clambered back on the couch, away from the abyss, fast, fast, fast. But she was gelatin, clutching, nails digging.

Her body went rigid, and she fought for breath.

Oh, God. Oh dear God.

His face looked different. No longer friendly, no longer benign, no longer handsome.

He opened a book that seemed to materialize from nothing, a sleight-of-hand to the crescendo of carnival sounds. Its appearance heightened the panic she felt, and her fingers dug deeper into the fabric of the tiny haven from the deep void that yawned beneath her.

Her mind began to double-track, attempting to focus on several things at once, yet unable to separate any one of them, to make any sense of them, or assist in her own salvation. The music was ensnaring her, some pounding preternatural cacophony.

Felicia Vanson *saw* words begin to pour from his mouth. They rode the music, a swath of letters and words that stretched from his lips, across the empty blackness that separated her from him, and entering her head by force, penetrating her.

"Red, roll rose bones
Truth hold no regard
The mind leads one way
Go but hold not
No good   fingers too slow
Exist in time

Die to build the priory
Patchwork construct prism
kaleidoscopic nothingness
                    the void"

He began to speak more quickly, more forcefully, raising his voice above the music's swirling undercurrent.

"This is our Time of Need
 Save us   Point the way
 I await the coming
 Speak to Me!
 don't leave me alone here
 I know Him Who Was
 arrested   held inside naked
 stale and wretched
 Put flame to this place
 Down black throat reach
 tear hard against its heart"

The words came so fast, so thickly from him that she tried to throw them off. But the sounds, the letter-word-bridge penetrating her was too compelling, too demanding, overwhelming her with profound confusion. And he kept on reading like a fevered preacher from a Holy book:

"Incandescent blazing fire
Words on Fire   World on Fire
Listless brittle pillars
Grand Hotel   Brothel
listen for the lions

roaming vacant fields   Forgotten
Predator
Speak to Me!
Unerring wings
carry the ferment   Someone
comes today who Knows
they comprehend but cannot say
like children
gnawing on the brain stem"

Each utterance was evoking an image, a picture in her clogged and cluttered mind.

Stooooppp! Stooopp. Stop.

Time was lost.

At the center of this cruel and pelting storm of words and images, she struggled to catch each breath. The outpouring of words etched indelible scars in her mind. Felicia felt her head filling up, with no outlet for the pressure roiling within.

She stared, horrified, into the couch-abyss.

She looked at the man she had once considered beautiful. Eyes she had found so compelling glowed with brilliant blue fire. Insane.

Noooo... Moorre... Please, please no more...

His rushing litany continued, his voice rising again now, demented, driven by unseen demons:

"Who tended the labyrinths?
Knew the Gods
Knew Dionysius   Knew me
These parable offerings   Hold on

to your breast and cleave
Drisk   Brume   Squalor
fumes meander the Quarter   Swimming
the tide for food
scraps to feed the children
Bells crook a finger   Tempt
inhabitants of the chasm
Come Here
come to Hell"

Felicia could no longer distinguish between the words, she felt and saw every single image careening off them. Like thick smoke, like clothes in many layers, each one too tight, his words and the swirling music smothered and invaded her. And paralyzed her.

"Listen   hear our voices
Long from the other Side
pay now
The devil has arrived
Hold fast your Secret
walk the pulpit
Scour the city   Stake claim
to ravage someone's daughter
Lift the cloak   And
the serpent shall reveal
to all amid the smoke and burning
Slip back to lethargy"

Breathless and sweating now, panting, in post-orgasmic

exhaustion, his chest rose and fell in wild rhythm.   Perspiration formed along his hairline and pressed the dark curls wetly against his skin.

His expression still burned with some inner possession.

He stood and floated down the hall, then reappeared holding something, reverently, in his graceful hands. Felicia strained her eyes around her fear, all she had left to call her own, but was unable to see across the vast, cold distance.

Carnival music pulsing again, a cascade of colors that fell like stars into the darkness beneath her. The same darkness upon which her host- tormentor floated.

The air was thick.   The sounds were thick.

Screeeaaamm...   Nothing. Nothing.

"You're so very lucky, Felicia, that I chose you," he said. "You will make a very special gift."

She had felt every image, and this one overwhelmed her. She stared, riding the swirling music. A black velvet bag, from which he now withdrew a long blade. He ceremoniously placed it beside a matching...*what do they call those things...* a chalice, also gleaming in the candlelight.

It was to be a part of her, she knew; she knew this as she watched, entwined on smoke and sound and echoing word. She tried to move on flaccid limbs.

Pleeaasse... please someone help me.

"I have one more reading for you, before you go, Felicia." His voice was serene as he imagined the taste of her coppery blood on his tongue. "They're the words of Jim Morrison."

He cleared his throat and intoned:

"As the body is ravaged
the spirits grow stronger

*Forgive me Father for I know
what I do."*

"Have you ever tasted blood, Felicia?" He asked calmly.
And she knew that her end had begun.

Chapter Seven

I CAUGHT THE FIRST SHUTTLE OUT OF AVALON, picked up a gutless rental car and arrived at Parker Center just as the detective shifts were changing. I didn't have to wait long before Hans Yamaguchi pushed his way through the glass doors.

"Well, son of a bitch. You came back."

"You knew I would."

Hans shrugged.

"You're just in time to see what we can get from Cal-ID. They were so goddamn backed up that they weren't able to get to it until this morning."

I followed him up the stairs to his desk. He spent about thirty minutes looking over his messages, then phoned down to the ID tech and told him we were on our way.

Cal-ID is a statewide computer network that contains a database of fingerprints that number several million. The main source of these records is the booking of arrestees into jail; however, when a person applies for a job that requires fingerprinting, such as one with the State of California, or one with a license requirement, the prints are run through the Department of Justice to determine any prior criminal history on the part of the applicant. The prints then also become a part of the vast State of California identification system.

"If we're real lucky," Hans said as we rode the elevator up, "Jane Doe's been printed before."

"Let's hope. I hate having to use the papers." If we found her in the system, it would only be a matter of hours, even minutes. Otherwise, we would have to bring the media in on the Jane Doe, publishing her photograph in the newspaper and soliciting the public's assistance in identifying the victim. That could take weeks and still give us nothing at all.

"Roger?" Hans addressed the tech. "This is Mike Travis. He's working with me on this one."

He reached out his hand without rising. "Roger Preston." He was new since I had left the job.

"Good to meet you. Got anything yet?" I asked.

"I found four possible matches, and requested their cards," Roger began. "Three were from the Department of Real Estate, and one from Social Services." When a potential match was found in the database, hard copies of the original fingerprint cards were obtained from the appropriate agency, then manually compared by the fingerprint technician to rule out any incorrectly identified persons. The computer could only match a finite number of data points.

"One of the cards had already come in, but it's not your Jane Doe. The others'll be faxed over any time now."

Hans nodded. "Who were the hits?"

Roger pivoted his swivel chair. "Paula Sanford, Lisa Jackson and Steven Morton, in the Real Estate system, and Patricia Courson from Social Services. Morton's out, obviously not female. And I ruled Jackson out when her card came in. The other two should —"

The technician's fax line rang and we all watched the machine expectantly. Within seconds the paper emerged and was immediately scrutinized by the tech. "Paula Sanford," he informed us. He took a small optical instrument that looked like a jewelers' loupe, held it between the thumb and forefinger of his right hand, pressed it to his eye, and studied the printed page.

Hans left to get coffee, while I stayed to watch. I found the procedure much more interesting now than I had when I had a desk full of active case files waiting for me downstairs.

Hans returned to the cubicle in time to see the tech turn back in his rolling chair to face us.

Roger Preston shook his head. "No go."

While we waited, I asked Hans about the door-to-door canvass of the neighborhood near the crime scene.

"Everybody's deaf, dumb and blind. But we've got a couple of ATM surveillance tapes. Kemp's got the new guy, Townsend, looking those over."

"Anything?"

"Haven't heard. But I can't imagine Kemp finding something and not thumping his chest loud enough for us all to know about it."

Preston's fax line rang again. He took the printout and examined it as he had the one before. Three long minutes passed amid the constant jangle and buzz of activity in the other cubicles. Hans and I remained expectantly silent.

"That's the one," the tech said, tapping the printout with his index finger. "Patricia Courson. I'll make you a copy of the card, and you can get on your way."

Hans and I took the card to the Homicide detail, and Hans took up a seat in front of the Model 40, the department's computer terminal that linked us to the databases of the Department of Justice, the NCIC, and the Department of Motor Vehicles. He entered the victim's name and date of birth on the keypad.

"Let's see if anyone's reported her missing," he said as he hit the return key.

There is a moment when a case becomes somehow more contemptible and horrible than it was at its inception. That is the moment when a Doe gets a real name. In this case, a 19-year-old coed from Fullerton, California, who had recently volunteered at a retirement home, requiring her to get fingerprinted. She had been a student at UCLA, living at an address in Westwood.

*   *   *

HANS and I arrived at the three story wood-frame-and-stucco apartment complex on Gayley Avenue, not far from the campus of UCLA. Once considered a safe-haven from the street crime and random violence common to South Central and East LA, Westwood was now just one more zip code to be violated.

Los Angeles was slowly eating itself alive.

The apartment building was indistinguishable from the structures on either side of it, situated on a rectangular lot, much deeper than it was wide. In front, Washingtonia palm trees sprouted from dirt squares in the uneven concrete sidewalk. It looked like it was from the late 1960's or early 1970's, and resembled an efficiency motel. If I had a daughter, I would feel relatively secure in knowing she lived here. Of course, looks can be deceiving.

The wrought-iron gate was propped open, and apparently stayed that way unless someone took the time to purposely latch it. The entry opened onto a rectangular courtyard. There was a fairly clean-looking swimming pool in the center. We located the first-floor apartment door labeled "Manager," and knocked.

"Whaaat?" An annoyed voice rode over the sound of a television.

"Police. We need to speak to you," Hans said.

That usually gets a rapid response. Sometimes they even open the door. Sometimes they run. There was silence for a moment, then the sound of the TV being turned off, latches of the door locks being turned.

A slight, red-haired man in his late thirties wearing a used-to-be-white undershirt and orange shorts appeared. His yellowish eyes squinted in the harsh daylight, a stark contrast to the gloom inside the apartment.

"Sorry to make you miss your show," I said. "What was it, *The Price Is Right*?"

"Yeah. You like it?"

"No. Are you the manager here?"

"Yeah. You guys have some ID or something?" he whined.

Hans reached into his jacket's breast pocket and pulled out the leather case that contained his detective's shield and laminated ID card.

Though I still possessed the shield of a retired detective and a permit to carry the Beretta 9-millimeter that I kept in a holster tucked over my right hip, I made no attempt to identify myself.

I had no *official* status; at least not until Hans got it cleared by the lieutenant.

"What can I do for you?" the manager offered, standing straighter, his eyes grudgingly accepting the daylight.

"Do you have a tenant by the name of Patricia Courson?" my partner asked.

"Patti? Yeah, uh, she and her roommate live on the second floor toward the rear of the building. Two-sixteen. What did she do?"

"Nothing. We just need to see her apartment. Do you know if her roommate's in?"

"I don't know, but I can get you a key if you need it." Mr. Helpful. Can't wait to find out what nefarious acts have been going on.

"No, that won't be necessary right now. Can you give me the name of the roommate, please?"

"Sure, just a minute. I'm gonna have to look it up. The lease is in Patti Courson's name, so I don't really remember." He went back into the gloom.

There were sounds of drawers opening and closing, paper shuffling, then he returned to the doorway. "Lori Snyder."

"Thanks," I said, "we'll be back if we need anything."

"Yeah, sure, okay. Anything you need." He left his door open, and stood in the doorway to watch what would happen next.

We climbed the concrete stairs to the second floor. All of the apartment units had their entry doors under a partially covered walkway that overlooked the courtyard. Small windows on each side of the door.

We approached number 216. I knocked.

The knock was a courtesy. Under the circumstances, we

had the authority to enter anyway.

There was no answer, so I knocked again, louder this time.

"Just a minute! God *damn!*" Our day for cranky apartment dwellers.

The face of a sleepy-eyed, dark-haired girl appeared at the window. She held back the curtain, squinting into the late morning sun. The sound of a chain-lock scraped the other side of the door, a deadbolt, and the squeak of the warped door being pulled open over a bent metal threshold.

The girl stood about five feet eight inches in her bare feet. She had long, deeply suntanned legs and wore an oversized tee shirt as a nightgown. Dark nipples showed clearly through the white cotton fabric. I attempted to maintain eye-contact. With her eyes, I mean.

"Lori Snyder?" Hans asked.

"Yeah. *God*, what time is it?"

"We're with the police department, Miss," said Hans, again offering his identification. "I'm Detective Yamaguchi, and this is Mike Travis." He nodded toward me.

"Is your roommate Patti Courson?" he continued.

"Yeah...what is this, anyway?" Suspicion replaced her drowsiness.

"I'm sorry," I said this time, and I was. "But your roommate has been found dead. May we come in, please?"

Her eyes went blank. She stood back. Then it hit.

"Oh my God..." and she physically backed into the room, clutching herself around the waist.

I looked over my shoulder, through the metal railing. The manager was still standing in his doorway. He gave me a thumbs-up. I shook my head and followed Hans into the apartment.

We immediately made a cursory tour of the apartment in an effort to identify whether there were any other victims, or perhaps the perpetrator him- or herself, waiting inside to do further harm.

It was a two-room affair, neat, with fairly expensive matching furniture. A faded tan carpet covered the entire area, except for the kitchen. It had beige linoleum. Framed poster-art decorated the walls and a live potted palm tree stood in the corner beside the sofa. The place was nothing like the dorm rooms and apartments I had shared during college.

On the coffee table was a ceramic ashtray containing a half-smoked joint.

After the brief once-over Hans and I returned to the living area where Lori stood waiting, arms still clutched tightly around her, as if she were cold.

"Can I get you a glass of water?" I asked, as I moved toward the kitchen.

I saw Hans reach into his jacket to retrieve a small dictaphone. He depressed the "record" and "play" buttons and recited the date and time of day. Satisfied that it was working properly, he took a seat on the couch, activated the recorder and placed it on the coffee table in front of him.

Lori said nothing, just sat down hard on the sofa and stared blankly.

"Oh my God...." she said, mostly to herself. "I can't *believe* this is happening." Hands and arms pressed against her stomach.

I found a glass tumbler, filled it with cool tap water, and handed it to her.

"Thanks," she muttered underneath her breath.

"Does anybody live here besides you and Patti?" Hans

asked.

"No. Just us," she answered.

"Do you know where Patti may have gone last night, Lori?" I asked.

"Uh...no...." She began to pick at the red polish on her thumbnail, a first small step on the journey back from shock. "She had a date with some guy. She was all excited. Look, I don't know....Patti and I don't really check in with each other, you know?"

"So you have no idea where she went, or with whom?"

"No. Just that it was some older guy from a class she had. That's all she said to me, anyway. Like I said, we weren't best friends or anything. We just roomed together, you know? My God, I can't believe this...." She was beginning to tear up.

"Can you tell us a little about her, Lori?" Hans asked.

"Like what?"

"What was she like....Did she do drugs?"

"No, she was pretty straight." Tiny flakes of polish fell to the carpet as she went to work on the other thumb.

"Date a lot? Sleep around?"

"No.....um, like I said, she's...um, *was* real straight. She took her schoolwork real serious. She was kind of a priss really. Kind of a cheerleader-type. She dated now and then, mostly clean-cut frat-types. I don't know much about her sex life, you know? It's just that she seemed real straight about that kind of thing."

"Meaning...?" Hans prodded.

"Meaning I don't think she slept around, okay?" she answered in an impatient tone.

"How about money trouble. Anything like that that you're aware of?" I asked.

"Not that I know of. She comes from..." She drew a ragged breath and exhaled loudly.

"Take your time, Lori," Hans encouraged her, adjusting the recorder.

She regained her composure.

"I'm sorry. She came from money. Her parents live in Orange County. Most of the furniture here is hers, I mean, her folks bought it for her. It always looked to me like she got whatever she needed from her mom and dad."

Hans and I waited in silence.

"I just can't believe this happened..." Tears leaked slowly into her brown eyes.

"What about her family? Do you know about them? An address, maybe?" Hans asked.

"I only met her mom once. The dad I met a couple of times. They seemed okay, but I don't think Patti always got along with her mom so well. They live in Fullerton, I'm pretty sure. I don't know the address or anything...." Her voice trailed off.

"Did she seem upset or nervous lately?"

"No. I mean, like I said, she was excited about going out with this guy in her class, but not *nervous* or *weird*, you know?"

"Lori, how did you come to share an apartment if you don't know each other so well?" I asked this time, fitting right into the rhythm that Hans and I had used so many times before in interviews. I still had it. The *Kehau* seemed far away.

Lori wiped her reddening nose with the back of her hand. I went back to the bathroom and brought some tissues.

"Thanks," she said. "I answered an ad she placed in the student paper. She needed someone to share the rent with. We met once, seemed to get along pretty well, and that was pretty much that."

That was when she noticed the joint that served as the centerpiece for her conversation with two police detectives. She licked her lips.

"Look," Hans said looking at her squarely. "I have to ask you one more question, okay? Did *you* have anything to do with Patti Courson's murder?"

The word *murder* hit her physically. Lori flinched, then blinked. Color rose up her neck to redden her cheeks and runny nose. The look that accompanied it was shock, outrage. That was a good sign. For her.

"*Me?*" she cried. "Are you goddamn kidding! *Jesus Christ!* She was my *roommate* for God's sake!"

"I'm sorry, Lori, that's one we have to ask." I said. Her reaction had been genuine. "You've been very helpful."

"We're going to need to look around a little more now. We need to see her room, okay?" Hans said.

"Uh....yeah, sure, I guess." She was recovering from her outburst. Her eyes went to the ashtray again, then quickly back to Hans. "It's the room on the *right*."

While Hans and I began our search, Lori Snyder composed herself enough to stand up from the sofa and find her way to the phone that hung on the wall in the kitchen. She began talking in low tones interrupted by short, stabbing sobs.

Hans took Patti's bathroom, and I started in on her bedroom.

The small bedroom was neat and well-kept, its walls decorated with more poster-art, and several framed five-by-seven photographs of Patti busy living her life. One photo caught her mid-jump, arms raised above her head, yelling something, dressed in a blue-and-white cheerleading uniform. Another showed her with two other grinning girls, arms over one another's shoulders, in matching graduation gowns and mortarboards.

A twin-sized bed held a small collection of stuffed animals. It was flanked by matching nightstands, matching lamps. Over one shade was draped a maroon and blue paisley scarf. Each nightstand contained a drawer. I decided to start there, in search of a diary or journal, rather than the desk that sat beneath the window.

In the drawer of what I gathered to be the side she favored sleeping on, the side with the digital clock radio, I found a flashlight, hand lotion, two light-blue terry cloth towels, a bottle of nail polish remover, and a thick paperback book on interpreting dreams. No diary.

The second drawer contained another towel, under which was a vibrator. Still no diary.

Her desk was very orderly, dead center atop which sat a green shaded desk lamp, and a four by six framed family photograph of what was obviously Mom, Dad, brother and the family dog. Nice domestic snapshot. A family about to be wracked with grief within the next few hours.

A telephone/answering machine was on the corner of the desk. I pushed the button marked "re-dial" hoping to get extremely lucky and have the call picked up by Patti's new boyfriend, the guy that currently topped our list of suspects. I was hoping she might have made a call confirming her date before she had left. I punched the "speaker" button so that I could listen without using the handset. There were the sounds of ringing, followed by, "City and listing please...." I hung up. Patti had last called Information. I filed it away.

A red light on the phone was blinking. That could also be good. I pressed the button marked "Play."

"Patti, it's Mom. It's about seven p.m. on Friday...I guess

you're out...look...*please* call me when you get in, okay? I love you. Bye." *Beep.*

A male voice came next. "Miss Courson? This is Don down at Sunshine Alterations? Uh...your slacks and jacket are ready. You can pick them up any time...Bye... Oh, it's about nine on Saturday." *Beep. Beep. Beep.* The red light stopped flashing. No more messages. I opened the cassette door and removed the tape. We would listen to both sides all the way through later.

The dead girl's desk blotter was an oversized calendar displaying in large squares each day of the current month. On it she had recorded various due dates for papers, upcoming exams, and in one square, *BP's B-day*. The previous day's box was empty.

Next, I turned on the desk lamp, knelt down in front of the desk and looked across the smooth surface of the desk blotter calendar for indentations, some note she might have written.

I continued going through the desk drawers, and found an address book. The cover was adorned with a photographed array of colorful flowers. It was about two inches thick, and worn on the spine. My cursory glance through the book gave me the impression that she had used it for a long time. She had written many entries in pencil, with childlike penmanship. Later entries showed her more grown up, a more mature hand.

Hans had finished his search shortly before me, and was now standing in the bedroom's doorway empty-handed and shaking his head.

"Nothing. Makeup, toothbrush, aspirin, tampons. No prescriptions. How about you?"

"Couple things. Address book, message machine tape and a calendar. I'd like to get the Esda machine on the calendar," I said, referring to a device that can detect almost microscopically slight impressions made on paper from the pressure caused by writing on the sheets above.

"The Esda will take a few days, but we can get people on the address book right away. You got her parents number in there?"

I thumbed to the section labeled "C," and showed him the entry "Mom and Dad" followed by address and phone numbers for a telephone, fax and "Dad's office."

"Yep."

"Okay, then. Looks like we're done here. Let's get next-of-kin notified."

We returned to the living area and found Lori sitting on the sofa, chewing on the inside edge of her thumbnail.

"We're finished here for now," Hans said as he held out his business card.
"We appreciate your cooperation. If you think of anything we might want to know, you call me, okay? "

Lori Snyder didn't move, so Hans placed the card on the table.

She gave a brief nod and kept biting her nail. The ashtray was gone.

I began to pull the door closed behind us.

"So what happens now?" she asked.

I tucked my head back in the doorway, gave my best reassuring smile, and said, "We go to work. We find who did this, and put him away."

She looked at me as if I were a slow-witted child.

"No. I mean what happens now *to me?*"

I pulled the door closed as a stray cloud obscured the sun and I watched my shadow disappear.

Chapter Eight

THE AUTOPSY HAD BEEN SCHEDULED FOR TWO o'clock that afternoon, and Hans and I had just enough time to grab a quick lunch at Mama's Louisiana Kitchen, a New Orleans style restaurant I knew on the west side. We parked the city car in a lot about a block away and walked.

"Been a while since you were here last," Hans said.

"Over a year. My retirement party."

Hans smiled at the recollection. "Hell of a time, what I remember of it."

"Mama always takes care of me."

"She ought to. If it hadn't been for you, she could've been killed."

"Fucking punks," I said. "What the hell were they thinking trying to rip off a place like that? In broad daylight, too."

"Speeding. Goddamn meth-heads'll go completely medieval on you. Tear you to pieces. Worse than angel dust."

"Yeah, well those two get to let their scars heal in Chico prison for another couple years before they get to think about scoring again."

"You showed 'em both some pretty good whoop-ass," Hans laughed. "Damn near killed one, didn't you?"

"Had to. Asshole wouldn't stop coming at me."

A bus blew hot exhaust across the sidewalk as I opened the door to Mama's. Spicy odors of the French Quarter permeated the air. The din of conversations and silverware. The place hadn't changed a bit.

"Mama's" real name was Berthamae Franklin, and she was probably between sixty and sixty-five years old, though I don't know anyone who knew for sure. She stood about five-two, weighed a solid one hundred eighty pounds, if not a little more, and had skin the color of polished walnut. She was always laughing or smiling.

"Why looka there!" she said loudly, with a big toothy grin. "Whachoo doin' back here, boa?" She threw her arms around me and squeezed me tight. Several customers' heads turned.

"Busy as ever in here I see," I said.

"Come on and let's get you a seat. Move some'a this riff-raff outta the way if we hafta." She playfully smacked the arm of a man seated at the counter.

She waddled through the groupings of deli-style tables, paper placemats set at each place. Bottles of red and green Tabasco, Crystal, and Cajun Red pepper sauces stood beside chrome napkin holders, and a plastic basket of utensils served as centerpieces.

She found an unoccupied booth, and gestured for Hans and me to sit. Mama handed over two big plastic-coated menus. Before we had a chance to look them over, she returned with two oversized plastic tumblers, filled to the brim with iced tea and a fresh sprig of mint. She stood patiently, hands on her ample hips. It took only seconds to make our selections. Mama took back our menus and went to place our order.

After taking a gulp of the tea, I stood, took a dollar from my khaki slacks, and selected a couple of tunes by *Beausoliel* and *Evangeline* on the jukebox. Michael Doucet's Cajun fiddle filled the room, adding the final touch of New Orleans to the ambiance. I returned to the table and slid back across the Naugahyde bench. I was instantly wary. Hans had his pulpit face on.

"You'd better go easy on Kemp if you're going to see this thing all the way through, Mike. He'd just as soon raise hell with the lieutenant and have your ass off this case," Hans said.

"I hear you. I just can't believe he's still around, that's all. Let's leave it there, huh?" After a couple of beats, I asked, "How long before you can get me official?"

"End of the day, all things working right."

"Great."

A stack of dishes and silverware crashed to the floor, and the place erupted in spontaneous applause.

"After the autopsy, I'd like to go back down to the beach, look at the scene again," I said. "That okay with you?"

"No problem. But you'll need to go alone. I've got to get the lieutenant brought up to speed, catch up with the rest of the investigative team. Gotta get some paperwork done. We'll need to reopen the 'war room,' get all the prior scene photos, evidence lists, timelines, all that shit, back on the walls, too. A lot to be done."

"Can you get me a copy of the killer's psych profile from before?" I asked.

"Yeah, sure. How about I drop you back at the office after the autopsy? You can pick up your car and go do your thing at the beach afterwards, and I can meet you when I'm done. How about six, six-thirty at Hinano's?

"Perfect."

Our lunch plates arrived, one heaping with rice and Jambalaya, the other bearing a soft-shell crab Po'Boy and a small mountain of cole slaw. The sandwich was mine. Health food.

"Eat hearty, boas. You need anythin', you shout, hear?" Mama said.

"Count on it, Mama," I said around a mouthful of Po'Boy.

Hans and I ate in a familiar silence for the next few minutes, enveloped by the sounds of the crowded restaurant.

"How's the retired life anyway?" Hans asked finally, his plate of Jambalaya half consumed.

"Hans, if I told you, everybody'd be doing it," I said. No point talking about the nightmares, the sweat-soaked sheets, the guns I still kept stashed in hiding places aboard the *Kehau*.

When we were finished, I folded some money and slipped it under my plate. As Hans and I reached the front door, Mama grabbed my arm and stuffed the bills back into my hand.

"You know better than that, Mike Travis," she said.

*   *   *

PATTI Courson's parents had already been to the Medical Examiner's office, at their own insistence, to identify the body. They probably hoped against hope that there had been some mistake. Their ordeal was only marginally less horrifying for them using video to make the ID, rather than seeing their daughter in person, laying in a sliding metal drawer. But they would never know that.

Hans and I arrived just after the identification had been made. Mrs. Courson weeping in the arms of her husband in the waiting area just outside the main room.

We walked through the double doors, and into the assistant M.E.'s cramped office. Papers, files, photographs, forms cluttered her gray metal desk. Unmatched four-drawer steel filing cabinets lined the back wall of her office. A computer, mousepad, and keyboard took up what little desk space was left. One of those sandbag stuffed animals, a big green frog, sat atop the monitor, legs dangling over the edge in front of the screen.

Her name was Dr. Sharon Ruffner, and she had occupied this office for the past nine years, having come over from some medium-sized burg in the Midwest whose name she had mentioned to me on many occasions, but I never remembered. She was a small-boned woman that I guessed to be about forty, had light brown hair, and horn-rimmed glasses. Sharon bristled with energy, moved like a bird, and had a direct, no-bullshit manner of speaking. I had worked with her on the last three of these serial cases.

She blew out a deep sigh from puffed cheeks as Hans and I walked in.

"Did you see the parents out there?"

"Bad," Hans answered.

"They hadn't heard from her since last weekend. Apparently she had had a fight with her mom, and hadn't yet made up."

The M.E. stood and walked into the anteroom leading to the main operating area to put on her scrubs, gloves and hair cover. She handed Hans and me a small stack of similar garb. Since

the appearance of AIDS, the days of Quincy cutting into victims without layers of protective clothing were over. Once we
had dressed ourselves, we followed her over to one of the stain-
less steel operating tables positioned along the wall to our left.
Nearly every one of the tables was occupied.

On my right was the body of a small child, maybe one or two
years old. It looked as though someone had boiled him like a
chicken.

Patti Courson's body was positioned on its back, stripped by
the criminalist of the clothes she had been wearing when we
had last seen her at Venice beach. The clothes would have been
carefully examined and booked into evidence. An assistant was
standing at the head of the table. One of his jobs would be to
photograph those portions of the autopsy that the doctor found
to be of evidentiary interest.

Sharon started by carefully studying the fist-sized blood
stain at the middle of the victim's sternum.

"There was no hole in the shirt matching this wound. Did
you notice that? This guy killed her, then *dressed* her. A lot of
blood loss, judging by her color, but we'll have a better idea
when we remove body fluids and stomach contents. The
absence of much of a stain on the clothing near the wound sup-
ports that, and I'm betting that the wound was not post-
mortem."

She turned back to the body on the cold metal table.

"Obviously a stab wound... double-edged blade, very deep...
no bruises on the neck... no marks on the arms or thighs.
Doesn't look like a junkie, but toxicology will tell us for sure."

She picked up the victim's left hand, removed the paper bag
that had been rubber-banded over it at the scene to preserve any
forensic evidence that might exist under the fingernails.

"Same as the other ones, guys: deep slice to the webbing between thumb and forefinger, and a deep slice across the ball of the hand. No abrasions on the wrists, ankles or neck, so it doesn't look like any restraints were used."

"Nothing else?" I asked.

"No apparent defense wounds, " she said finally, still frowning. "She wore a ring, but it's not here now. See the tan line?" she said finally.

Hans and I nodded.

"No defense wounds. No other cuts. Only on the left hand. *Very* unique," Sharon said.

She moved to the foot of the table and leaned in close to examine the body's pubic area.

"No abrasions. No visible bruising, or torn tissue. No apparent forcible rape."

Hans and I continued to observe and listen. A curious look passed over her face.

"Well, well..." she said after another moment's careful scrutiny. She motioned to her assistant, who positioned himself to photograph her new discovery.

"Forceps please," she said.

The doctor placed the forceps at the pudenda, inserted them, and withdrew a piece of paper carefully folded and refolded to about two inches square, from the victim's vagina. She placed it in a metal tray.

"That should be interesting," she said, looking me directly in the eyes.

"We'll need a copy to take with us," I said.

She had the assistant shoot us several copies before he bagged it for the forensic team.

*　　*　　*

I SAT alone in a booth in the back of Hinano's, a bar on Washington Boulevard, located near a dark but crowded parking lot. Beyond it was the sand of Venice beach. The surf was loud enough to drown out the low hum of surface street traffic. Inside was noisy conversation and the Allman Brothers' *Ain't Wastin' Time No More* on the house sound system.

The room was a large rectangle divided into two sections. One for billiards and the other for drinking and eating. Separating each section was the bar itself, covered by an overhang made of palm fronds. It reminded me of places I'd seen on the beaches of Mexico, or the South Pacific.

The female bartender was heavy-set with a short white apron slung about her waist. She was busy smoking, tapping ashes into an ashtray, and talking to a customer in a raspy voice.

I pulled a folded single sheet of white eight and half by eleven paper from my shirt pocket. It revealed an appalling piece of computer-generated animated "artwork" that depicted a naked young woman with shoulder-length blond hair, lying prone upon brown, cracked, rocky ground, with a deep blue sky giving way to ominous thunderheads in the distance. Spikes had been driven through open hands, crucifixion style, into the dirt. The agony on the face was beyond description.

From her back sprouted butterfly wings, that morphed into feathery angel wings near their tips. Her legs were widely spread. From her vagina emerged the head, front legs and torso of a large green iguana. In one clawed foot the creature clutched a long silver dagger, the other rested on the ground beneath its splayed claws. The lizard's mouth was partly open. Long, sharp teeth. A lolling wet tongue.

Something new. Something more sophisticated than before. A chance, however slim, to get at our killer. Previous cases had all included some form of visual communication, but nothing so detailed. The M.O. had been changing as well.

I was drinking an Asahi beer that I had poured over a tall glass of ice, and cracking peanuts from the shell. I began re-reading the psychological profile that had been prepared by the FBI, in conjunction with our investigative team, from before. Hans had taken the time to have a copy made for me after the autopsy.

After walking the beach and the crime scene, I had come to Hinano's as Hans and I had earlier arranged. I was settling into a comfortable rhythm: nut, paragraph, beer. The floor between my feet was littered with empty shells.

I closed my eyes, and tried to visualize the suspect being described in the paragraph I had just read, the person who had most recently re-entered my life by taking Patti Courson's. Nut, paragraph, beer.

Hans arrived at precisely six-thirty. He crunched over the spent peanut shells and slipped into the seat opposite mine. I held up two fingers, and got us another round of Asahi. Then he reached into his breast pocket and pulled out a shiny piece of plastic. It made a brittle, rattling sound when he tossed it on the table in front of me. A laminated ID.

"You're official," Hans said. "It took some doing — Kemp had already made a complaint with the lieutenant. Fortunately for you, the Loo knows Kemp is a whiner."

I rolled my eyes.

"Anyway, he continued. "You'll be getting a flat fee of two hundred dollars a day, plus an expense per diem of another seventy five. The per diem is to cover lodging and/or transportation — just keep the receipts."

"What about my nine?"

"Yes, you can carry your gun."

He paused a moment, then added, "Welcome back. Now don't fuck it up."

Vintage Hans. His favorite way of wishing good luck.

Our order arrived together with two fresh Pilsner glasses brimming with ice. Hans pulled at his beer and wiped the foam from his lip with the back of his hand. He reached into the red plastic basket and took a handful of peanuts.

"I don't like the profile anymore, Hans. There's something that doesn't sit right."

"I know. This Courson thing is different. He changes his M.O., but the signature stays the same. You can sense this guy has *reasons*. I just wish I knew what the fuck they were."

Psychological profiling is art as much as science, and as such, can easily be wrong. I felt the profile that had been developed based upon earlier information was flawed. We needed to reassess it. Take another look at everything.

"Certain things I can still buy," I began. "For instance, I still think this guy is intelligent, charming, probably good looking. There have been virtually zero *real* defense wounds. Only the deep cuts to the victims' left hands. That means the victims all *trusted* this guy... let him close to them.

"There's almost no similarity between the victims physically, and the *geography* of the murders still doesn't make any sense. The guy gets all the hell over the Country. But *why*? Why here? Why Miami? Connecticut? New Mexico? The victims didn't know one another, but they all end up apparently trusting this same guy... *shit!*"

Finding that connection was one of the most important keys

to the case. It was frustrating as hell.

"What do you want to do?" Hans asked, as he poured his beer into the tall glass.

"I want to take it to someone else, get a fresh perspective. Maybe come up with a whole new profile, start from scratch."

"How long?"

"Hell, I don't know. Maybe three or four days, a little longer. I'm thinking of Jacquie Whitney. What do you think?"

"I think it might be hard talking her into it," Hans shook his head.

"She does great work. One of the best forensic psychs we ever worked with if you ask me."

"No question. I'm just thinking that after that last case she did —."

"The pillowcase guy."

"Yeah, that one. They busted the guy right outside her apartment building. She went into private practice right after."

"Sick bastard," I said.

"Got that right. You think she'd be willing to work another serial case after all that?" Hans asked skeptically.

"I don't know. But she's as good as they get, Hans."

"Then give it a try. I think she's in Century City now."

I got her office number from Information, covered my ear against the noise of the bar. After three rings, I got an automated message.

"You've reached the office of Doctor Jacquie Whitney. I will be out of the office until Tuesday. If this is an emergency, please dial my service at five-five-five-nine-three-nine-three, otherwise leave a message and I will return your call as soon as I can."

"Hey, Jacquie, it's Mike Travis. Sorry I missed you. I could really use your help on something I'm working on with Hans Yamaguchi. Please call me as soon as you can, it's important." I left my cell-phone number.

Returning to the table, I said, "Message machine. Said she's out for a couple of days. But I can use the time anyway. I'll get in touch with her when she gets back, and run her through the case details if she agrees to help us out. I'll need an extra set of crime scene photos and notes from each of the victims."

"Okay. It should give me time to get the war room back up to speed, anyway. We should have the toxicology reports by then, and the full autopsy write-up, estimated time of death, and all of that. I can get the extra set of material for you then."

Hans nodded at the photocopied evidence I had tucked underneath the old FBI profile. "This is one sick fucking guy, Mike. And it looks like he's getting weirder all the time. You think he's getting sloppy? Desperate?"

"Dissembling? No. I don't think so. There's not much *violence* in the Courson murder, you know? No apparent *rage*— not like the first victim. That guy was cut to ribbons. I just can't figure what the hell he's up to. But, no, I don't see him dissembling. If anything, it's getting more *dis*-passionate."

Hans stared into his beer as if it held an answer.

"I'll tell you what's really bothering me," I said. "Where's he been for the last year? Why'd he go dark?"

"Maybe he got put down for something else, and now he's back on the street."

"Yeah, maybe." But I didn't think so.

"I really hate this motherfucker."

"We'll put him down," I said.

A hippie looking guy took a stool at the bar next to a young man in black leather and the heavy-set bartender started making a fuss with him about something. The young guy looked wired, and he waved his hands wildly as he spoke to the hippie. Hans and I looked over and watched for a minute while the young guy came out of pocket with cash for a drink that the bartender apparently didn't think he had. The young one slid the drink over to the hippie and things calmed down. Hans and I returned to our beers.

"You're welcome to stay with Mie and me," Hans said, referring to his very attractive, diminutive, Japanese wife, whose name is pronounced "Mee-ay."

"Thanks, but no. I'll get a hotel down here somewhere."

"But you gotta come over for the Fourth of July. It's only a week away, you know. We're having our annual barbecue."

I told him I would.

"Bring a date. The more the merrier."

I wondered how Deana would like being around a picnic full of drunk cops. "I'll do my best."

"Let's finish these beers up, then. I gotta get home."

I paid our tab and we walked out into the balmy evening. The sun had just begun to set.

I shook Hans' hand firmly.

"Give Mie a kiss for me," I said.

Hans nodded, turned and walked off toward the beachfront parking lot.

*   *   *

IT WAS still early, and I was too wound up to do much other than arrange for a room and try to drink myself to sleep. Outside on the sidewalk, I used my cell-phone to make a reservation at a hotel I knew just a block down the strand. When I was finished, I ducked back into Hinano's and took a seat at the bar.

I glanced at my watch and thought about Avalon. I could picture my friends at Pete's; Dave, Rex, Ponytail Mike, the Singin' Dude. And Deana. I could still smell her perfume, and how she tasted when I kissed her. It all felt so far away.

The bartender slid my Asahi across the counter and I laid a twenty down in front of me. I swiveled around on the stool and leaned my back against the bar.

A Beretta nine is a big chunk of steel, and prints easy on your jacket. So you move carefully. You watch your body language. After a while it gets to be routine, but I guess I was a little rusty. Sharpen up, Travis, or somebody'll take you from behind, make a grab for the gun.

The network news glowed noiselessly from a TV overhead and music blared from speakers in every corner of the place. I tried to clear my mind of the multitude of details that swirled around inside me, and think about nothing.

The sound of rainfall filled the room, followed by the cocktail lounge strains of the Doors doing *Riders on the Storm*. Jim Morrison's smoky voice sang:

> *There's a killer on the road*
> *His brain is squirming like a toad...*

"Great song, man." It was the young guy in the leather jacket from before.

I looked left, then right, to see who he was talking to. The hippie was gone. It must have been me. I nodded. "Yeah."

He had one of those rare faces that defied my ability to place an age on it, but his eyes had the edgy look of a speed freak at the long end of a three day jag. I watched him throw back the remains of a straight whiskey and light a fresh Marlboro from the butt of the old one. Smoke poured out his nostrils as he signaled the bartender for another round.

"He used to live down here, you know? Slept on the roof of an old building over by the beach." The guy gestured toward the door, the cigarette wedged between his fingers.

"Hmmm," I said, not knowing what the hell he was talking about. He searched my face for comprehension and looked even more agitated when he found none.

"Morrison, man. He dropped acid and wandered around down here alot," he nodded vigorously. "Right here in Venice Beach."

"You don't say." Right here in Venice, home of the walking weird. Who would've fucking guessed?

"No kidding, man. People said that he was, like, possessed. But he wasn't. My mother knew him real well."

The guy reached into the pocket of his black jacket and pulled out a pair of dark glasses. He ran the fingers of one hand through long curly hair and slid them on top of his head.

I took a pull of my beer and looked out toward the night.

> ...*If you give this man a ride*
> *sweet family will die*
> *Killer on the road* ...

"Wanna know what I think?" The guy said.

No. "What?"

"I think he was from a whole other time, man."

He waited for me to respond, but I said nothing.

"Dig this," he continued. "They say the spirit of an Indian

shaman jumped into Morrison's body when he just was a kid traveling through New Mexico."

"Why don't you leave this guy alone, huh?" The bartender intervened, wiping her hands on her apron. Her expression was screwed up in a look of disapproval.

The young man's face went hard. "Why don't you fuck off," he answered through clenched teeth.

"It's no problem," I said to her. I had to admit, listening to the guy ramble was more entertaining than living inside my own head. The woman shrugged and waddled back to her cigarette.

"Thanks, man," he said.

"Sure."

He squinted at me. "Hey, don't I know you?"

"I don't think so," I answered firmly. I guessed that my picture had been in the paper in connection with the Courson case.

"Hmm," he responded, then changed the subject. "How about spottin' me a drink? I'm a little short." His leather jacket creaked as he patted down his pockets.

"Help yourself," I said, and gestured toward the twenty on the bar. What the fuck.

I ignored him as he waited for his refill and I drifted into the music.

> *... The world on you depends,*
> *Our life will never end ...*

"Fuckin' genius, man," the young guy interrupted again.

"Yeah." I said, looking away.

He drummed the bar with his hands, keeping time with the

music. "What a fuckin' *trip,*" he grinned wildly.

"I'll bet."

The song rode out in a rumble of thunder and rain. I was ready to call it a night. I tossed back the last of my beer, picked up my change, peeled off a five for a tip and gave it to the bartender. I handed the speed freak the rest. "Here. Knock yourself out."

Chapter Nine

EARLY THE NEXT MORNING, JACQUIE WHITNEY returned my call.

"A voice from the past," she said playfully. "To what do I owe the honor?"

"Some old business, Jacquie."

"Police business? But I thought you retired."

"I did, but Hans called me back to assist on a case. The Patti Courson murder."

"Young girl? Found on the beach?"

"That's the one."

"I saw it on the news this morning." An edge crept into her voice. "Not that I'm not glad to hear from you, but what does that have to do with me?"

"We think it's part of the serial case we were working a couple of years ago. We could really use your help."

There was a long hesitation. I heard the passing of a siren in the distance.

"Jacquie," I pressed, "I remember why you went into private practice, and I wouldn't ask you except there's nobody I trust on this kind of thing as much as you."

"What's your time frame?"

"As soon as possible. We're thinking this guy may be gearing up again."

"I wouldn't do this for anyone else, Mike. I was taking a few days off." She agreed to rearrange her plans for later that morning in order to accommodate me, gave me directions to her new office, and rang off.

After a quick breakfast, I drove over to Parker Center to pick up the case files from Hans. I figured I had plenty of time to refresh my memory before my meeting with Jacquie.

He was standing beside his desk, a small sheaf of papers in his hand, talking to Dan Kemp.

Kemp's look was measured, cautious. I had pull, I had my plastic ID, I had my carry permit, and I had my reputation.

"I was just leaving," he said.

I watched his back, thinking I'd better watch mine. "Have a nice day, Dan."

Hans ignored the exchange. "We got Patti Courson's class listing from UCLA. Administration over there is going to help round up as many of her classmates as they can. I'm going over to interview them now. Wanna come along and give me a hand?"

"Can't. Jacquie Whitney's meeting me in a couple hours. I came to get the case files."

"Shit. I guess I'll take Kemp." He handed me a stack of manila file folders from his desk. "Here are your files. Two sets, hot off the copier."

I thanked him and started to leave.

"One other thing," Hans said. "I talked to the parents and got a description of the missing ring."

"Yeah? Get it out to the pawn shops yet?" I asked.

Hans shot me a look.

"Just asking. How about boyfriends? Did her parents have anything for us?"

"If there were, her folks didn't know about them."

*　　*　　*

I ARRIVED at a group of identical black-glass office towers, arranged around a fountain courtyard. On the twenty-second floor, a perky young receptionist greeted me from behind a rosewood desk.

"I'm Mike Travis, and yes, I have an appointment," I said.

"Just a moment please, Mr. Travis," she dropped her eyes and spoke into the microphone of her headset..

"She'll be with you in a moment, Mr. Travis. May I get you something to drink — coffee maybe — while you wait?"

"Hot tea if you've got it."

She unplugged her headset and walked off.

I stood at the window while I waited. The sky over Century City was brown and thick with a layer of smog that often accompanied hot, windless days. Looking down, I got a nice aerial view of the courtyard and fountain, and watched scores of suit-clad employees carrying briefcases, purses and files.

The first time I had met Jacquie Whitney she had been working another serial homicide that had terrorized the Hollywood area for about a year and a half. I wasn't working that case, but it was a nasty set of torture-murders of homosexual males that turned out to be the work of two killers working together. Jacquie had been the only profiler who had suggested that there might be two perpetrators and not just one. She took flak for that. But her insight had provided a breakthrough on the case.

She was an attractive redhead with a smooth peaches-and-cream complexion, about five foot four, slender and athletic. She had a grace that belied the trauma and violence to which her work exposed her.

Her deep green eyes would sometimes glaze as she assimilated details on a case, her mind configuring and re-configuring possibilities. She had told me once that she first wanted to know as much as possible about the victims, how they lived and what their habits and personalities were like, so that she could "become" the killer. To understand from the inside what made one particular victim more desirable than another in the eyes of the predator. From there she could intuit and form a useful profile of the kind of person who would select a certain type of victim and behave in a certain way.

I heard a door open behind me.

"Good morning, Mike. I see your yacht has been treating you well. How long has it been?" said Jacquie's familiar voice.

"Too long. Over a year."

"You do a lousy job of keeping in touch."

"It's good of you to see me on your day off, Jacquie. I really appreciate it."

"Anything for you and L.A.'s finest, you know that, Mike. Come into my office and we can talk."

I retrieved my files and followed her into an elegant office offering a floor-to-ceiling view of West Hollywood.

On one side of the room was a simple but expensive rosewood desk, fronted by two oxblood leather wingback chairs. A couch, glass coffee table, and two matching barrel chairs creating a less formal seating area. A crystal vase contained dark red antherium, protea, and bird of paradise. The office smelled like leather and new carpet.

"Let's sit at the table, that way we can look at your files together."

I followed her lead.

"So, what do you think of the new office?" she asked, obviously enjoying the trappings of a lucrative private practice.

"It suits you perfectly, Jacquie. Very elegant. Those flowers over there. The crystal vase. Those paintings —"

"You like them?"

"Very much. Jan Kasprzycki, right?" I said.

Her eyebrows went up impishly. "Impressive. What happened to the beer-and-peanuts man I knew?"

I grinned. "He's still around. So who pays the bills for all this?"

I took a seat on the comfortable couch and placed my thick set of file folders on the table in front of me. Jacquie sat in a barrel chair.

"Corporate clients mostly. Psychological profiles on potential employees. They send candidates to me for an evaluation, not just skills and intelligence, but more subtle things such as their ability to handle stress, motivation, problem solving, that sort of thing. It's difficult to terminate employees these days. Better to pay me than to make a mistake that could end in a lawsuit."

"Looks like they keep you busy."

"They do, knock wood." She paused, gesturing at my file folders. "So what's happening, Mike. You know I haven't done a murder case profile in a while."

"Just have a look. You can make up your mind after you've seen what I brought."

A knock on her office door was followed by the entrance of the perky receptionist. She carried a silver tray with a carafe of coffee, another filled with hot water for me. There was a wire basket containing a selection of teas.

"Will you be needing anything else, Doctor Whitney?"

"No, that will be fine, thank you. Please hold my calls, unless it's an emergency, okay?" Jacquie said.

Perky nodded, pulling the tall wooden door closed behind her. I tried to imagine what would constitute an "emergency" in Jacquie's new line of work.

I selected a tea bag, steeped it. "We've got a series of murders that have taken place over a period of four years. I'll start from the beginning, and leave you with the crime scene notes and photos if you want them when we're done. Feel free to interrupt or ask any questions of me if I neglect to mention something you consider important, all right?"

"Let's do it."

"The first murder had actually been among the last to be identified as part of this series of killings because it had been so different from the others. The body of a forty-four year old Caucasian male, a non-commissioned Army officer, was found beside Interstate 10 on an isolated stretch of desert between Santa Fe and Albuquerque. The man had been stabbed twenty six times in the chest and torso. A hand written note that said 'Forgive me Father, for I know what I do' was found in the pocket of the uniform jacket that the victim was wearing when he was found."

Jacquie grimaced. "Lovely."

"At the autopsy it was determined that the killing blow had been a deep wound that penetrated the solar plexus and entered the heart. The remaining wounds had been made post-mortem, possibly as much as two to three hours after the wound that caused the victim's death. The penetration of the heart had been made by a long-bladed, double-edged knife. The remaining wounds by a different blade.

"There were two deep slashes on the victim's left hand, originally thought to be defense wounds. As you'll see in a minute, these later assisted us in identifying that victim as a part of a series whose other victims bore strikingly similar marks on the hands.

"The forensic people were able to pick up two hairs from the body, both different from one another, as well as some cotton fibers."

I had spread the photos of the dead soldier across the table as I described the details of the case. Jacquie looked carefully at each one in turn. I watched her green eyes darken in concentration as she scanned them. I sat in silence, waiting for her to break it.

"God, I forgot how bad these things could be."

I said nothing. True enough, the mangled body didn't go well with the rosewood decor.

"The body was dumped there?" she asked after two or three minutes.

"Yes."

"Any idea as to where the actual murder could have taken place?"

"Not really. The time of death was estimated to be sometime between midnight and two o'clock in the morning. The time of discovery was about ten o'clock in the morning that same day.

The murder could have been anywhere, though, given the delay in time between the initial stab wound and the post-mortem mutilation."

I lifted the tea bag from my cup and placed it on a saucer.

"It suggests to me," I continued, "that it was someplace where the killer felt he had the time to wait, a place where he felt safe. I believe it's probably a vehicle, like a van. But the problem is that we didn't find any carpet fibers or other forensics to corroborate that."

"And of course the hairs are worthless without someone to match them against...." she said as much to herself as to me.

"We did get a match on one of the hairs. It matched some that were found on two of the later victims. So I can tie the victims to one obvious common acquaintance but I can't find any further connection between them."

"Any signs of torture or restraints being used?"

"No. And there was no homosexual angle either."

"Anything missing from the victim?"

"A brass button from the uniform jacket, but it's impossible to know if it was lost in some sort of struggle or taken as a keepsake by the killer. My money is on the latter."

She rested her chin on her hand, temporarily lost in thought. I took a sip of tea and waited.

After a few moments, she said, "Okay, who's next?"

"The next one was found about two months later, in a rental car parked in the lot of a motel near the Phoenix airport. The car turned out to have been reported stolen by the rental agency earlier that same day.

"This time, the victim was a thirty-year-old divorced black female, a flight attendant on layover out of Sky Harbor and staying at the hotel. She had one deep stab wound to the heart, deep cuts and some bruising on the left hand. One earring was missing.

"Again, there were no signs of restraints being used or sexual activity, abusive or otherwise. A note written in pencil on the inside of a motel match book read: 'My dusky jewel.' It was found in a pocket of her blouse."

I spread the crime scene photos in a second row.

"A search of her hotel room turned up nothing. According to the Phoenix P.D., the hotel had been extremely busy during the week preceding the murder, and the hotel staff had little time to clean the rooms thoroughly. There were too many fingerprints, fibers and hairs from too many different sources to prove of any use. A blood toxicology report concluded that she had a blood-alcohol level of approximately point two-two and she had been pretty much out of it."

"What about blood tox on the first victim, the Army guy? What was his story?"

"Sorry. There was a fairly high alcohol content with him, too. Quaaludes, as well."

"Drugged or a user?" she asked.

"According to family and friends, he drank some, but drugs were out of the question. His doctor confirmed that he hadn't prescribed any. You never know, though."

"They checked the flight attendant's ex-spouse...." she said, not exactly a question.

"Yes, but his alibi was tight."

"What about her fellow flight crew at the hotel? What about them?"

"All of their stories checked out with corroborating witnesses, and none had spent any time with her after arriving together at the hotel."

"What was the victim wearing when she was found?"

"Slacks and a blouse —"

"No, I mean *underneath*."

"Panties, but no bra and no shoes. Her feet were clean, so she obviously didn't walk to the car."

"No other mutilation?"

"None."

"The handwriting on the notes was the same as before?"

"Close enough to say yes."

I spent the next hour outlining the details of the remaining victims. Jacquie examined each crime scene photo with exacting care, making notes to herself on a white legal pad.

The third victim had been a sixty-four-year-old, wheelchair-bound retired cop, in Miami, Florida. He had been found in his home by relatives the day after his murder, the family having failed to hear from him by telephone as they normally did. That time, the circumstances looked like a home-invasion scenario, but the cause of death was a single stab wound to the heart with a double-edged blade.

This victim had ligature marks on both wrists. Fibers collected at the scene were examined by the forensics unit. It was determined that they came from a popular brand of women's panty hose.

The same cuts as those found on the first two victims were present on his left hand, and this time a tooth had been extracted from the victim's lower jaw. The dentistry had been done post-mortem, and no further mutilation was in evidence.

No unfamiliar fingerprints had been found at the scene, but tiny particles of what turned out to be the same as the powder used in surgical gloves had been found on and about the victim's wrists and forearms, leaving us to conclude that the killer had come prepared to kill, and was wearing gloves.

Jacquie rubbed the bridge of her nose and closed her eyes. She got up and walked to her office window.

"You okay? Want to take five?"

She returned to her seat and leaned forward. "Go ahead. I'm ready."

The fourth one had been committed in Hartford, Connecticut under circumstances decidedly similar to the murder in Miami, though the victim was a white twenty-seven-year-old female, a 911 dispatcher. This time another hair was found, and matched the hairs found on the first victim.

The fifth was a twenty-two-year-old call girl found just out-side the door of a bungalow at the Chateau Marmont in Hollywood. The bungalow had been reserved, then canceled, and was supposed to have been vacant. She had also been killed elsewhere, then dumped. Cause of death was a single stab wound to the heart by a double-edged blade.

Sixth was a twenty-eight-year-old stripper found on a dirt abutment beside a small parking area behind the Hollywood Bowl. Same M.O. and same cause of death.

The seventh victim was a twenty-one-year-old UCLA coed found under a tree in one of the many park-like areas around the huge campus. She had been a third-year student in the film school.

Number eight was Patti Courson.

Jacquie leaned back and looked at me. The pages of her notepad ruffled against her skirt. This time her green eyes were warm. "More tea?"

"No, thanks. I'm fine."

Her hand came up and she went through her notes. "I'm going to have a few questions. But first, the restroom. Then I need to check my messages."

"Okay." I said I would do the same.

A few minutes and we were back at the table with our problem. We arranged and rearranged the photos until at least one photo of each victim was visible to her while she reviewed her notes again.

"So we've got eight murders, all by a single deep thrust of a double- edged blade to the heart. Each has some bruising and deep cuts on the palm or the web between the thumb and forefinger of the left hand. All but two of the victims seem to have been dumped. Dumped *outdoors*, in public and semi-public places. Each has had some sort of message found with the body, either a short phrase, or 'artwork' of some kind."

I nodded. "Right."

"Now for the artwork," she continued. The warmth had left her eyes again. "It has become more and more sophisticated as time has progressed, but each possesses very violent, sexual and surreal content. None of the victims have shown evidence of sexual abuse or assault, and only two show any sign of having been restrained — both of these are also the exception to the rule as to having been killed and dumped elsewhere. So, the signature is the same, while the M.O. has varied."

"That's correct."

The tapping of her pencil was loud. She was deep in thought, in her own world.

"The victims don't have any connection to one another. And there's no significant similarity in age, gender or race."

"Unusual for a serial case."

"Absolutely," she agreed. "The geography is interesting, but appears concentrated in the Los Angeles area most recently.

"Patterns are going to require some work. But I don't see

any connection with the dates of the murders. They weren't all done on the fifth of the month, or every thirty-two days, or only on Tuesdays and Thursdays..." she trailed off.

I waited.

"There *is* a recurring theme of *metamorphosis*, though — the butterfly/angel wing imagery," she went on after a moment. "The lizard is a repeated visual as well. I really need to think on that, but it says something to me about *change* within the killer's psyche."

She tossed her pencil on the table.

"It troubles me, though, Mike, that the guy was inactive for over a year, year-and-a-half before this most recent case."

"I've been thinking about that, too," I said. "It's possible that he could have been arrested and put away for something, something minor, and just got out."

"Could be," she allowed. "Could also be that he's been somewhere else killing other victims you just don't know about. Just like before."

"I don't think so. The details of these cases has been on the books for a long time, Jacquie. I can't see something with characteristics like our guy's going unnoticed, or uncompared to cases elsewhere in the—" I stopped myself.

"It could happen, though," she persisted. "The first four homicides had taken place one per jurisdiction. They wouldn't necessarily see it as a part of a serial crime."

"I'll see what I can find. If he's been quiet this long, though, what would you make of it?"

She shrugged. "This is really challenging, Mike. Let me think on this overnight, and call me tomorrow morning. I'm usually in the office by seven or seven-thirty. If I have any questions in the meantime, should I use the number from before?"

"That's my cellular. I almost always carry it with me."

As if on cue, it rang. It was Hans, and I told him I would call him back.

I got up. "I really want to thank you for this. I know it is a big imposition on you, but we've got to find him."

"Or her. Got to keep an open mind."

"Or her."

I left a duplicate set of case files and photos with her, and gathered mine.

"Are you going to be okay with this, Jacquie? With the stalker thing from before?"

"If I wasn't, I'd tell you, Mike. I'll be all right."

"Okay."

*   *   *

ONCE I GOT off the elevator and outside to the courtyard, I punched in Hans' number. He answered before the second ring. I told him that we should have someone look into out-of-state homicides to see if we could find where our guy had been for the past year and a half.

"Is she okay with helping on a case like this?" Hans asked.

"Says she's fine."

"Good. One more thing: we've got a meeting with Loo and the rest of the investigative team at eight-thirty tomorrow morning."

"I'll be there."

I found a small sandwich shop in an office building adjacent to Jacquie's. I took an outside table and ate an egg salad on whole wheat while looking over the case file.

I had a hell of a lot of reading to do.

Chapter Ten

HE HELD THE BLOWTORCH TO THE GLASS BOWL of crystal meth in the pipe positioned between his fingers. He was careful not to let his dangling hair get caught in the bright blue flame. He drew deeply, held the expanding gas in his lungs for as long as he could stand, then exhaled. The hair on his scalp prickled as he was nearly overcome with a rush of ecstasy.

The threnody of drums and bass emanating from the stereo in the next room seeped through the thin walls of the mobile home he had rented. He smiled, deeply satisfied with his accomplishments thus far. His mother would be proud.

His brain squirmed and darted in celebration over the events of the preceding weeks and months; at having eluded the authorities; but more importantly, having moved both physically and spiritually closer to his exquisite purpose.

The rental of a mobile home in a north Orange County

enclave of surfers, blue collar workers and retirees had been the linchpin. He could operate freely. The lease was paid up six months in advance. In cash.

It seemed that he had caught them at exactly the right time, desperate and anxious to be rid of the monthly burden of maintaining the mobilehome that had once been the retirement residence of the husband's elderly parents, now both deceased.

The LSD was just beginning to come on too, and together with the ice he had smoked, he was almost ready to kneel before the dark altar of his insatiable benefactor. A narco-sacrament. It broke the bonds of the corporeal world and entered closer to the ethereal.

The world of the spirit — eternal, mystical and open only to those with the courage to seek, and to sacrifice. One had to be strong, committed, and unrelenting, if one were to attain the ultimate gift.

He thought of himself as *The Changeling*. As suitable a name as any he had ever been given, or taken, but much more fitting now.

Fuck, yeah! Bring it on!

His eyes cast about. Neat, organized, everything in its place. That was the way he liked it. The way things needed to be.

Furniture and decor had been left entirely intact. He had modified only one room, the only one to reflect his true nature. If anyone were to enter unexpectedly, the rest of the place would look as if an octogenarian were still in occupancy.

He put on dark glasses now. The combination of acid and ice made him very sensitive to light. Even through the mirrored lenses, though, he saw brilliant flashes — strange and wonderful images and colors — as his mind writhed and contorted. He felt the familiar dual sensations of total reckless abandonment and complete control. .

A sexual thrill shot through him suddenly, and he felt him-self grow hard in anticipation of what came now.

Time for vespers.

Chapter Eleven

THE MEETING OF THE INVESTIGATIVE TEAM WAS
scheduled to begin at eight-thirty, but I decided to arrive
early to meet with the lieutenant, and see if I could give Hans
an assist. The Homicide floor hadn't changed since I left: cluttered and battered desks, the forms, files and garbage generated
from the tragedies giving livelihoods to its occupants. The polished linoleum floor reflected the blue neon. The air smelled of
burned coffee and men's cologne.

I rapped on the door frame that surrounded the lieutenant's
frosted-glass door. He was sitting at his desk reading the contents of a manila file folder. He looked up and motioned me
inside. We hunched forward and shook hands in the cramped
space.

The lieutenant was a tall, broad shouldered, dark-skinned
black man of about forty-five. He had a short-cropped head of
black hair, graying at the temples. His name was LaFayette

Delano, but he preferred to be called "Loo" as in "Loo-tenant." I guess when he became a Captain, he'd want to be called "Cap."

"Hello, Mike. Good to see you again. Been a long time." His voice was deep and raspy. A dedicated smoker.

"How are you doing, lieutenant?" I asked.

"Doin' okay, doin' okay. So, it looks like maybe your boy is back at it."

"Looks like it. I looked in on the Courson autopsy with Hans. It's our guy."

Loo reached into his pocket and pulled out a pack of gum, offered me a stick.

I shook my head. "You quit smoking?"

"City building. Can't smoke in here anymore." He peeled the wrapping off the gum and popped it in his mouth. "I'm not going to bullshit you, Mike. Dan Kemp has already been up my ass about you. I really need you to go easy on him. If he starts writing complaints and shit, look — I don't need any more hassles, okay?"

"I hear you, Loo."

"Good. Now welcome back to the big dicks. See you at eight-thirty."

Evidently, I was finished talking with him.

"Thanks. See you in a bit," I answered.

I made for the break room to brew myself some hot tea. I could hear the morning arrival of detectives through the break-room wall.

*   *   *

THE conference room had been turned into a 'war room,' with

scores of bloody crime-scene photographs pinned to rolling tackboards the size of grade school chalkboards. Across the top of each were long rectangular pieces of paper printed with the name of each victim, and the date of that particular murder. Several of these boards were positioned around the table so that everywhere you looked, the victims confronted you, challenging you to find their killer and prevent the addition of others to their numbers.

A map of the United States was pinned to another rolling board, and had stick-pins with numbered, triangular flags protruding from the site of each homicide. The map looked like a golf course. And a golf course looks like a cemetery.

In addition to the Loo, Hans and me, there were three other detectives in the room: a Homicide veteran named Robert Bobb (a.k.a. "The Man With No Last Name"), Dan Kemp, and someone new to the detail named John Townsend. The latter three had handled the majority of the field interviews so far on the Courson case.

Styrofoam cups of coffee were filled, consumed and refilled throughout the meeting. A pink box of doughnuts sat open in the center of the table; only one remained, and the meeting had just begun.

"We picked up the surveillance tapes from the three ATM's in the area of the body dump. I looked over the tapes, but got nothing," Townsend began.

"You watched them all?" Loo asked. "Front to back?"

"From the estimated time of death until the time the body was reported," he replied.

"How about the days prior to the dump, are they on the tapes you got?"

"Sure, those time-lapse tapes probably have a week's worth

of pictures at least," Townsend said.

"Might be a good idea to look at 'em again. Let's see what else we've got," Loo said, then directed his next question to Kemp.

"How about the neighborhood canvass?"

Kemp answered, "Sir, I talked —"

Bobb shot him a hard glance.

"I mean *we* — talked to every business owner within three blocks every direction from the pier, and got nothing. No unusual activity, no 'new customer' frequenting the area, nothing. Nobody saw a thing."

The lieutenant nodded, unsurprised.

"Hans, what about the UCLA interviews?"

"I spoke with the admissions and curriculum people to get Miss Courson's schedule of classes," Hans explained. "Then interviewed each of the professors, and obtained a list of the students in each class. We've located and interviewed about two-thirds of the students so far. In any event, we're getting a pretty consistent picture of the victim: conservative, reserved, good student, and apparently not too close with anyone we've talked to as yet.

"On a related note," Hans went on, "we've got the victim's telephone records for the last week of her life. I've already talked with the roommate to see if any of the calls were hers. A couple of them were. We *do* have one other number that we'll run down. It was made earlier the same day as the murder."

"Good," Loo said. "Any boyfriends you can find?"

"Nada. The only information we have about her dating habits is from her roommate, Lori Snyder. Mike and I talked to her the day of the call out. According to Miss Snyder, Patti Courson dated infrequently, and her roommate didn't have any names for us. Mike found a calendar in her bedroom with some writing depressions on it. That was submitted for Esda examination to see if it'll cough up any numbers or names, and Kemp's working on the address book from the apartment. Maybe something will turn up there."

"What about the parents?" Loo asked.

"The only boyfriend they knew of was from her high-school days, and that's been over for a while, according to them. We checked it anyway, and it turns out he's been in Europe for the summer. His parents sent him. It checks out."

"Must be nice," Bob Bobb said sardonically.

"We'll keep looking. Like I said, we've got about a third of the classmates to get through yet," Hans said.

"Okay. How about blood toxicology?"

Bobb answered. "Blood alcohol was point zero six. She might have been a little buzzed, but under the legal limit. There was no evidence of opiates, methamphetamine, or cocaine either. That's the first-level screen, but I've asked Dr. Ruffner to go back and do a full screen. We'll see if anything else shows up there. It'll take another day or two."

"Fine. Anything else?"

"Yeah, forensics found some cotton fibers that don't match the clothing found on the victim. And also some hairs that are not hers. Lab just tested the hair, and sure as shit, it's the same as the ones from three of the other victims: number one, number four, and the soldier."

"Bullseye," I said to smiles around the table. It was now scientifically confirmed that this was the same guy who had committed at least four of the eight known murders, and would be important evidence when we caught the killer and brought him to trial. It would be extremely difficult for the defense to explain the presence of a defendant's hair at four separate crime scenes, in three different states, all bearing similar causes of death and M.O.

"Prints?" I asked hopefully.

"Zilch," Bobb said.

"Well, the cotton fibers have shown up before," I said. "But we all know they're damn near useless. I wish this asshole wore synthetic clothes."

"I don't follow," Townsend, the new guy, said.

"Man-made fibers vary significantly from one manufacturer to the next. That makes them alot easier to identify and compare," Hans said.

"And juries love that kind of shit," Loo added. "How about you, Mike?"

"I love that shit, too, Loo," I said.

"I meant —-"

"I know what you meant. I've reviewed the case files again in detail over the last couple of days. I've spoken with Dr. Jacqueline Whitney about the case, and she has agreed to provide us with some input on a profile."

Before anyone could interrupt, I held up my hand and continued, "Now I know somebody may get a hard-on over having to pay for this, but I feel pretty strongly that we need a second opinion. A fresh perspective might generate some questions or insight that we haven't considered yet. I don't know the cost yet, but when Jacquie's looked the case files over, she'll debrief me —"

"I bet she'll *de-brief* you," Kemp said.

"Put a fucking sock in it, ass-wipe —-"

Loo stepped in. "All right, knock it off. Kemp, you've got a career to think about. Travis, I got you some plastic that I could just as easily pull."

The table got tense.

"Like I was saying," I said slowly, "she'll go over her pre-liminary take on things with me, including what she's going to charge. At a minimum, it will either confirm the profile we've got already, or it'll provide some food for thought. I should be hearing back in the next day or so."

"I don't disagree, Mike, just keep the team plugged in," the lieutenant said.

Hans said, "Before we split up, I'd like to take a look at the latest correspondence from our freak here." He had set up one of the tackboards with a chronological arrangement of the com-munications that had been collected off the victims.

The "notes" had been enlarged to eleven-by-fourteen inches, full color, in three rows. Left to right, they displayed the work of a psychopath. Our challenge was to decipher the "message" being sent, make some sort of sense of it, and predict the next likely step in the progression. Hopefully, this would be done in time to prevent the death of another victim.

The upper left corner of the board exhibited a highly enlarged photograph of a piece of lined notebook paper, the kind that could be bought by the gross in any drug store, that had been torn into quarters. The quarter sheet that had been found in the pocket of the first victim had been folded into quar-ters again, after having had *"Forgive me, Father For I know what I do,"* written in block letters, with a number two pencil. Beneath this photo the name of the first victim, Steven Paul Carp, had been carefully printed with magic marker.

To the right of this was a similar-sized photographic enlarge-ment of the inside cover of a hotel matchbook, upon which had been written *"My dusky jewel,"* also in pencil, and again in block letters. It was obvious to everyone present that each of these had been written by the same hand, despite the simplistic effort to defeat handwriting analysis by using block-style letters. Again, the victim's name had been placed underneath the photo: Sophia Fern Nicholls.

The third, and final, glossy print on the uppermost row showed a full sheet of plain white paper, copy machine paper, upon which had been typed: *"Pigs. Filth. Wealth. Sex? Nudity? Death? What is obscene?"*

This time, the note had been pinned to the shirt of the victim with a safety pin, and had come off a computer printer.

The lab had pegged the model as a Hewlett-Packard Desk Jet, an unfortunately common and affordable printer that had been available to the consumer market for some time. We could not track the note to a particular machine.

The fourth enlargement was the first of the drawings that had appeared with the victims. It was a simple pencil sketch, marginally better than average quality, depicting a butterfly. Beneath this sketch were the words *"The Scream of the Butterfly,"* again typed in block capital letters, using the same computer printer. This note had been carefully folded and placed into the victim's mouth.

Hans had the floor. "I'd like to hear some thoughts as to what we think might be going on, what he's trying to say. I know we've been through these before, but I was thinking something new might come to mind by viewing them chronologically, and with the Courson note in place. Any thoughts?"

The room remained silent as each of us stared at the grotesque collection.

The door to the conference room swung open.

"Sorry to interrupt," the Division's administrative assistant said. "But I've got a couple of messages here that I thought you'd want right away. They just came in." She looked directly at Hans.

She handed two pink squares of flimsy message-pad paper to him, and closed the door behind her. Hans looked at each in turn, then looked up at the expectant faces surrounding the table.

"Seems the Esda machine kicked back what looks like a phone number, Mike. Good catch," he said nodding his head toward me as he spoke my name. "The sequence is two numbers short of being complete, but we've got something to run down at least."

Hans waved the second flimsy. "We've also got another apparent victim. We ran the case details through the interstate network again, like Mike and I discussed yesterday. This one happened about three months ago in New Orleans. Looks like the coppers down there missed the hand wounds, among other things. The victim is a thirty-nine-year-old black female, found under a footbridge across from Jackson Square. The file is on its way."

"This one have artwork, too?" I asked.

"Looks like it. That's what turned their lights on down there, when I mentioned the notes and artwork we've been finding on the bodies," Hans answered. "But they didn't tell me what it was yet. It'll come in with the case file. They're faxing it as we speak. Hard copy will follow in overnight express."

The meeting was about to conclude, and the new information needed to be immediately acted upon. Hans turned to Kemp.

"Dan, you take this number and get all the possible names and addresses from the reverse directory. If you don't find them there, call the phone company and get them. We need to talk to every person whose number this could be until we find a connection with the Courson case. I think we can start with the assumption that the area code will be the same as that of Miss Courson's apartment, otherwise she would likely have written it down with the number...."

Hans walked to a white dry-erase marker board and wrote the number that had been detected through the use of the Esda machine.

5<u>2</u>?- 30<u>2</u>3

With the third and sixth digits missing, that left a maximum of a hundred possible names and addresses. That is, if all of the possible digits between zero and nine were currently in use as legitimate telephone numbers. Even Kemp could probably handle that.

"Bobb," Hans said, "you and Townsend finish up the student interviews. I'll stand by for the New Orleans file, and we can get back together after we've worked the new dope. Loo, any objections? Anybody got anything that won't keep for a few hours?"

"No objections here," Loo said.

"Just one thing, Hans" I said. "I want to look those ATM tapes over. You've still got the copies the lab made, right Townsend?"

"Yeah, sure. They're in my desk. I'll bring them in." He looked glad to be relieved of them.

"That copacetic with you, Loo?"

"Fine with me, Mike. Okay, let's reconvene this little party day after tomorrow. Same time. Good hunting."

The room cleared rapidly, but I stayed behind to look at the array of communication provided by the man who had left a trail of nine bodies. Nine that we now knew about, anyway, and who showed no signs of stopping. As I looked at the photos and notes, I asked myself the same question over and over, like a mantra: *What is he trying to say?*

I positioned myself directly in front of the tackboard displaying the enlargements, leaning on the scarred conference table. I took up where we had just left off.

The fifth victim, the young call girl found outside the Chateau Marmont, had been found with a more sophisticated drawing than the one before. This one featured the image of an angel, wings spread behind gauzy, flowing robes. A brilliant red heart shone through the angel's gown, as if it were glowing from within. The face was somewhat androgynous, wearing an expression that could only be described as puzzled or angry. The medium was pencil and watercolor on artist's watercolor paper. The paper was so ordinary that it was untraceable.

This had been the first communication of its kind in the case, though it proved to be a precursor in style to those that came later. It was the first to feature only artwork, with no accompanying verbiage. This had also been the first one to contain color, not just images or alphabetical characters on common white paper.

I closed my eyes and cleared my mind in preparation of observing the next image. When I was ready, I looked.

This one represented another "first." It had been generated entirely by computer, and had been printed, as before, on the H-P printer. It was a full page of 8 1/2 x 11 inch paper covered in its entirety by a "wallpaper" image of reptilian skin, variegated in hues of deep green and yellow-green. It was like an extreme photographic closeup of an iguana or some similar lizard. Again, no written message accompanied it. In many ways, this one had been the most puzzling.

I involuntarily shook my head, and shifted my attention to the next photograph. This bit of evidence had been found folded into eighths, and placed inside the panties of the seventh victim, the UCLA coed named Pamela Descanso. What appeared on the page was another computer-generated fantasy: a reptilian "hand" clenching the thick handle of what appeared to be a sword or dagger. The form was so enlarged as to make only the handle and the hilt of the blade visible, before it disappeared off the top edge of the paper.

I tilted my head for a closer look at the Courson "note" and noticed that the Descanso artwork was actually a closeup or "detail" of the reptile's clawed fist that now appeared in the most recent murder.

I felt a small twinge in my stomach, the first in a long time.

*   *   *

I HAD been viewing the ATM surveillance videos for about two hours, careful to keep my attention focused on the outer edges of each time-lapse frame. I was looking for anything we could use to identify our killer: a parked car, a profile, anything. All we had so far were his bizarre communications and a likely window of time during which Patti Courson's body had been dumped.

Since most banks use and re-use the same video tape, the one I was viewing was expectedly low in quality, compounded by the fact that its purpose is primarily to photograph the ATM user. As a result, the background information was both distant and blurry. It took a lot of concentration to stay focused on my task.

According to Townsend, he had previously viewed the tapes, beginning at the coroner's estimated time of Patti Courson's death through the time that the body was discovered on the beach. While that was logical, I knew it would be worth a try to see whether a broader time horizon captured by the video would yield anything useful.

I took each of the three banks' videos, and viewed them in one-hour increments, as indicated on the time code that was displayed at the bottom of each frame. After watching one bank's tape for a certain sixty-minute period of the day, I would then switch to the next bank's tape for the same period, and so on. While this was mind-numbingly tedious, I wanted to get a feel for the activity of the area throughout the course of a typical day.

I clicked off the tape, and stood up. I was ready to take a break when my cell phone rang.

"Mike Travis," I stated after the third ring.

"Mike...this is Deana." The line was noisy, but I could hear the smack of billiard balls in the background. "Look," she continued, "I just wanted to say thanks for the other night. I'm sorry if I was kind of a bitch, but I wanted you to know that I really enjoyed being with you."

Both the call and the content took me by surprise.

"No apology necessary. Forget about it."

"I'm at work right now, so I can't talk long. It's just that... God this is *so* difficult. I just wanted you to know that I.... I didn't want you to think I was a total bitch is all. It was nice of you to care enough to even ask about me. About my life."

"Deana..."

I wasn't the best at this kind of conversation, either. I wanted to tell her I missed her. Long seconds ticked by.

"Hello? Are you there? Mike?"

"I'm here. When I get back to the island we'll do it again, okay?"

"I'd like that a lot, Mike, I really would. And I've been thinking about what you said." There was a pause. More static on the line. "Look, I gotta go.... Thanks again," she finished in an awkward rush.

"I'll see you when I get back."

"I hope so. Bye, Mike."

"Bye," I said. Avalon was only twenty five miles across the channel, but it never felt so far away.

*   *   *

I HAD just finished viewing all three bank video tapes, and my head was pounding. I looked at my silver-and-gold Tag Heuer diver's watch, ascertained that it was four o'clock, packed the tape copies into my briefcase, and retrieved the keys to my miserably underpowered rental car.

It pisses me off to spend money on things that will bring me no pleasure. Driving in L.A. is a miserable fucking experience at any hour of the day, in any kind of car. Call me frugal.

I slipped the Beretta into its holster and adjusted it for my drive back to the hotel, paused briefly in front of Loo's door, and mock-saluted my departure.

"Travis?" He waved me back in.

"Yeah, Loo."

"I came down a bit hard this morning. In front of the team, I mean."

"Forget it. I shouldn't have let Kemp weasel me."

"It's the pressure. We're all feeling it."

I nodded. "'Night, Loo."

"'Night."

The Pacific View Hotel did, in fact, have a view overlooking a small stretch of the ocean. My room had one of those views.

After over an hour of commuting the twenty-something mile stretch from the Homicide division to the hotel, I bypassed the valet and self-parked in a narrow space in the underground garage. In the lobby, I was caught by the sounds of a piano drifting out of the bar in the back.

I stopped by the concierge desk to check for messages. None. Of course, the only person who knew where I was staying was Hans, and he had my cellular number, just like everyone else.

As I ascended to the sixth floor in the hotel's glass elevator, I tried to pinpoint the source of the niggling feeling of having overlooked something important. I assumed it originated from my fruitless, though methodical, examination of the tapes, but I couldn't be certain. Over the years, I had frequently listened to my inner voice on matters such as this.

Experience had taught me that the best way to coax anything productive out of my nagging inner voice was to engage in something physical. Something that would take my mind off the matter at hand. I put on a pair of jogging shorts, running shoes, and a tank shirt. I checked myself in the mirror as I taped a small Beretta Minx pistol under my sock and departed the hotel for a cheap fix of endorphins.

I had no destination, but I gravitated to the foot of the Venice pier, about two miles away. The oppressive heat that had enveloped southern California over the past week had dissipated, but I was soaking nevertheless.

I cooled down by walking the length of the pier, enjoying the cool sea breeze. I watched the waves approach the pilings beneath me, then roll on to break noisily on the white sand of the beach behind me.

The sounds of children laughing mixed with the cries of seagulls. A cool mist wafted in the wake of crashing waves. The sounds spoke to something inside me and calmed my unsettled self as I made my way back the way I had come, to the foot of the pier.

I stared at the spot where Patti Courson's body had been found.

Where is the sonofabitch now?

I walked over to the spot on the sand where I had first seen her, and stood silently, imagining that it was dark, picturing what it must have looked like in the early morning hours as she was being left on the beach to be discovered by strangers. I looked around to locate the nearest lights, and tried to imagine how much of it would have penetrated the dark stretch of beach between two key points of light: at the street corner, and at the foot of the pier.

The body had to have been driven to that spot. Patti Courson would not have been too heavy, but it was not easy walking with any kind of a load over dry, loose, deep sand. The killer had to have parked close by.

Where?

The only logical spot was the corner where I had first arrived at the scene, having at the time been occupied by police and related emergency vehicles. The only potential problem was the position of the street light that would have lit the car from above as the killer made his drop. But there would have been no alternative. He needed the shortest distance between his transportation and the dump site to avoid the risk of detection, not to mention the physical demands placed on him by the load he carried. I was sure of it. It had to be *right there.*

I walked to the spot at the dead-end formed by the street and the thick wooden guardrail that separated it from the beach itself. I stood in the gutter of the curb, just where the tires of the killer's car must have been, and looked around in a three hundred and sixty degree circle.

There.

The People's Bank of Venice. A direct view, albeit diagonal across a short intersection not one hundred feet from where I stood. Theirs was one of the tapes we had. I had watched it. But I must have overlooked something.

A charge of adrenaline surged.

I started to run back to the hotel where I could concentrate my full attention on the Peoples' Bank tape. No distractions.

I flung myself through the door to my room, breathless and soaked with sweat. Yet the adrenaline rush overrode my discomfort. I located the Peoples' Bank video and fumbled it into the player. Winding the tape forward, I found the time and date code I sought.

My heart beat hard in my chest, but my eyes burned unblinkingly into the television screen.

And there it was.

I saw the badly blurred image of a vehicle, parked exactly where I had stood not twenty minutes earlier. It appeared in only fifty frames of video. Less than twenty-five seconds of total screen time.

Chapter Twelve

BEFORE I GOT IN THE SHOWER, I PLACED A CALL to the forensics lab. Experience had taught me that the lab knew no particular hours of operation; had technicians there at almost every hour of the day working on something.

I was fortunate to find that when I asked for my friend, Vonda Franklin, the forensic tech who specialized in photographic and video evidence, she was still there. She agreed to wait for me to bring the People's Bank tape.

Within an hour of my call, Vonda had made a copy of the tape section requiring enhancement, plus about two minutes on either side it. After returning the original to me, I showed her the frames where I needed her magic.

The focus was blurry, and the tape was now one further generation removed from the original. It compounded the difficulty of turning the muddy images into something serviceable. I had seen it work, though, using digital processing. Frames of photography nearly as indistinct as what I possessed, had been electronically cleaned-up to provide relevant information to an investigation. I could only hope for a similar break this time.

"Don't hold your breath, Travis," Vonda said. "This is real shit."

"I need the upper left-hand corner piece there?" I pointed to what appeared to be a front fender, tire and wheel of an automobile.

"Like I said, don't hold your breath. But I'll do what I can, okay? How about you come back late tomorrow?"

"No, no. No good. See, I need this *now*."

"Oh, balls. I can't do that. I mean, *damn it,* it's almost eight-thirty already. No. Forget it. I'm sorry." Vonda looked tired. I was sure she had been in the lab since early that morning. Still, if the evidence was to prove useful, every hour counted.

"Look, Vonda, there's a guy out there butchering people. The latest one was found in Venice Beach. Carved on, like a ritual. She was a college kid, her whole life ahead of her. We found her dumped, curled up alone on the sand."

"You shit, Travis."

"He's out there. That's why I'm pushing."

"Fourteen hours I put in today —-"

"I've got one little, tiny, minuscule fucking lead here, and *you* won't spend a *few extra hours* to help bring this motherfucker in?"

"C'mon, Travis, gimme a break here...."

"I'll give you a hand. I can help."

"*Right.* You — help?"

"Hungry?"

She hesitated.

"Pizza. Or deli sandwiches. On me."

She rubbed her eyes, and sighed.

"I've got a yacht in Avalon. How about a weekend away from all this? Clear blue water, sunshine..."

A look of resignation crossed her face. "Yeah, sure. Deal. Pizza *and* the yacht. For the record, the yacht did it."

By the time I returned with the pizza an hour later, a large deep-dish with Canadian bacon, pineapple and anchovies, Vonda had completed the first step of the process: digitizing a number of "still" photographs from the best of the frames of the video that we could find.

"Just in time," she said. "I've got the stills ready."

"Let me have a look."

I looked at the monitor.

"They're pretty dinged up and scratchy, but they're the best of the lot," she sighed, slowly scrolling through a series of four newly digitized pictures.

"What's next?"

"We use 'ERASER.' It's a program that will eliminate the scratches and marks off the picture. What it does," she continued, "is divide the image into about three hundred thousand tiny squares—"

"Pixels—" I interrupted, so as to indicate that I was not a *complete* techno-dumbass.

"Right. Pixels. Anyway, because the image is black-and-white, each of these pixels is considered by the computer to be a shade of gray and assigned a number between zero and two hundred and fifty. Zero is pure black, two hundred fifty is pure white."

"Uh huh."

"After each of the pixels is encoded, we'll ask the software to take the average gray-scale code all around the sides of the various marks and scratches, and use those averages to 'fill-in' the damaged part of the image. And..." She punched the keys on the well-worn keyboard on the desk in front of her for a couple of minutes. *Voila.* The image is whole. Scratch free."

"That's really amazing," I said admiringly.

Vonda nodded.

I put my hand on her shoulder. "You okay?"

"Yeah, just a little light-headed. But, I'll make it."

"I'll square this with you, Vonda."

"Damn straight you will."

Vonda saved the newly 'cleaned' version of the photo to a computer disk, so if anything went wrong in the next stages, we'd have something to go back to. When the sounds from the disk drive ground to a halt, she swiveled her chair around to face me.

"Let's eat," she said.

We moved to an unoccupied table at the rear of the windowless room, and made room for the pizza box and ourselves. I made for the vending machine against the wall, and dug into my wallet for a pair of one-dollar bills.

"Buy you a drink?" I asked.

"Thought you'd never ask. A Dr. Pepper."

I inserted the first dollar into the narrow slot and waited while the machine determined whether to spit it back at me. It did.

I dug into my wallet again, found the most pristine bill I had, and slid that one into the damn thing. The machine found it acceptable and allowed me to make my selections, then proceeded to keep my change. *Bastard.*

Vonda was on her second slice of pizza by the time I

returned with the drinks, and smiled at me as I approached.

"Machine get 'ya?" she asked.

"Sure as hell."

"He's a little fucker, isn't he? The machine I mean."

"Little bastard kept my change. Must be a tidy little profit center."

As I pulled a slice from the box, I asked Vonda what was next in the process with the video.

"What I'm going to try to do," she said, "is sharpen the focus on the pictures by finding a single point of light on the image to use as a 'focus.' The Feds used the same technology when Hinckley shot President Reagan."

"How's that?"

"What they did was use something in a photo of the shooting that they knew should be a *point* of light. In that particular case it was a reflection of the sun on the bumper of the limo. Because the picture was blurry, the reflection looked more like a *line* —"

"And the length of that 'line' is equal to the amount of blur on the image," I guessed.

"Exactly. So we condense the image of that *line* of reflection down to a *point*, and the rest of the image shrinks down right along with it."

"And you'll try the same thing with our pictures?"

"Right on. But that's only the next step. There's one more after that." She took another bite of pizza.

"What is it?"

"I manually manipulate the gray-scale. That way, I can create more contrast in the image."

"What's that going to do?"

"You never know. I've had faces, license plates, even printing on documents become visible in high-contrast. Other times? Nothing."

"What can I do to help?" I asked.

"Nothing. Just let me get this done. It'll take several more hours, so there's really no point in sticking around. Why don't you take off? Call me first thing in the morning, okay?"

"I really appreciate it."

"Go."

By the time I got into the rental car to make the return trip to my hotel it was already 10:30 p.m. It had been easy to lose track of time.

My brain was jangling. I knew that sleep would be a long way off if I couldn't create some semblance of order. I rolled down the window and let the rush of warm wind envelop me, listening to the hum of rubber against pavement. I shuffled the murders into groups, trying to find a pattern that still eluded me.

I recited the gender of each of the nine victims aloud, in chronological order. "Male, female, male, female..." the sound of my own voice trailed off. All the rest of the victims were female. No pattern, other than he seemed to be focusing on women. That was something.

Their ages. The first three were older than the remaining six: 44, 30 and 64. All the others were under forty. Though Patti Courson was the youngest of all of them, I couldn't see a pattern there either: 27, 22, 28, 39, 21 and 19.

I turned off the freeway onto Washington Boulevard and headed toward the beach.

"Occupations," I said aloud. "Army officer, flight attendant, cop, 911 dispatcher, call girl, stripper, waitress..." *And two UCLA coeds*. That was something new.

The bleeping of my cell-phone startled me.

"Travis here."

"You know The Whisky a Go Go?" Hans voice rode over the static.

"On Sunset?"

"We got another one."

I was already making a U-turn as Hans hung up.

*   *   *

HUNDREDS of people crowded the sidewalk in front of the club. Red and blue strobes from patrol cars bounced off walls. I showed my ID to the uniform behind the yellow tape and he waved me to the alley behind the Whisky.

Hans was already there. Kemp wasn't. Bob Bobb worked the perimeter of the crowd asking for witnesses. John Townsend was taking a statement from the busboy who found the body. I nodded to Townsend and strided over to Hans who was staring down at the body.

She was naked, propped like a rag doll against a metal dumpster. Her legs were splayed to reveal a message that had been carved into the flesh of her inner thighs. *I am the Lizard King.*

"Nice," I said. "Cuts on the hands, too?"

"Yeah."

"Anybody know who she is?"

"The manager says he's seen her around the club before. Doesn't know her name," Hans said bitterly. "But he thinks she works around here."

"Any idea how long she'd been there before they found her?"

"Less than an hour and a half. The busboy said he was out here on a smoke break then."

"By himself?" I asked sharply.

"No. He checks out. He's got three other employees that say he was in their sight all night long."

I squatted on my haunches and looked at the body. "Looks like some bruising on the wrists and ankles."

"Notice anything else?"

"She's still got her jewelry on," I answered.

"Check out the necklace," Hans prompted.

A gold pendant in the shape of a heart hung from a chain and rested between her breasts. Just above the bloodless slit where I knew we would find that a double-edged blade had penetrated her heart.

"Jesus," I whispered.

I had never actually seen it before, only had it described to me. By the family of the fourth victim. Lacy Costello, the 911 dispatcher from New Haven. Twenty seven years old. Tied up with her own panty hose and killed by a dual-edged blade that punctured her aorta. The necklace had been a gift from her grandmother.

Bright camera flashes pierced the night.

Chapter Thirteen

THE TELEPHONE RANG AND WOKE ME FROM A troubled sleep.

I reached for the source of the noise atop the nightstand.

"Good morning, Mister Travis. It's seven-fifteen. This is your wake-up call," said the cheery young voice on the phone.

"Uunghh..."

"Have a nice day."

Willing myself from the bed, I dropped to the floor and did one hundred pushups followed by an equal number of sit-ups. It got the blood moving.

The hot shower reddened my skin and started to bring me back to life. During the four hours I had slept, I must've had a dozen dreams, each one a jagged shard in my subconscious. I felt irritable. Dogged by something I couldn't put my finger on. Something the guy in the leather jacket from Hinano's had said about New Mexico and Jim Morrison. As a cop, I had never believed in coincidence, but I didn't know what I was supposed to make out of the ramblings of a speed freak.

I emerged from the shower about the time room service arrived with my breakfast. I wrapped a towel around my waist, admitted the white-jacketed waiter, added a tip, signed the chit, and saw him out. Between bites of poached eggs, sliced papaya and whole-wheat toast, I punched out Jacquie Whitney's office number.

After ringing three times, her perky receptionist answered. "Doctor Whitney's office."

"Good morning, Is Jacquie there? This is Mike Travis."

"*Oh*. She's on the phone right now."

"I'll wait."

"Ohh- kay."

I punched the speakerphone button on the hotel telephone so I could eat my breakfast while holding for the popular Doctor Whitney.

I switched on the television and found CNBC. I trimmed the volume to a bare minimum while I waited for Jacquie and watched the stock ticker. I thought of my dad and his preoccupation with the market, with money. It left a shadow like a passing cloud.

In my mind I saw Deana on the veranda of my family's house. *"Being a cop is a long way from Wall Street..."*

Then I thought about our brief conversation the day before. The sound of her voice.

My stomach felt queasy. I was agitated. Restless. Unsettled. Something....

"This is Doctor Whitney," came the voice from the telephone's speaker. The TV screen went black as I punched the "off" button on the remote.

"Morning, Jacquie. This is Mike Travis."

"Good morning to *you*."

"Have anything for me yet?"

"Some feedback for you, but nothing written as yet."

"No problem. What'd you come up with? Should I come to the office?"

"No, no need for that. I'm booked all day. But your call was perfectly timed. Want to go over the basics right now? On the phone?"

"Sure. Shoot. Just give me a second to get some paper and a pen. I want to take some notes. Mind if I keep you on speaker?"

"Not at all. I'm going to give you my observations in no particular order, though. By the time I write it up, it'll flow much better. But for now, why don't we just jump in?"

Her voice sounded hollow and disembodied. "First off, did you check about the period of inactivity?"

"Yes, we did. There was another victim. Black female, late thirties, in New Orleans. There was more artwork found on the body, but I haven't seen it yet. Happened about three months ago right in the middle of the dormant period."

"Sorry to hear that. But I'm not surprised. My take is that these crimes are part of some sort of ritual, almost ceremonial —"

I interrupted her. "There was also another one last night, Jacquie. No ID yet."

"*Damn* it, Mike." She exhaled audibly. I knew this was what she didn't miss about her old job.

"I just thought you should know. Let's go ahead."

"Right. Well, aside from the first victim — the one in New Mexico — the killer has taken pains to treat the bodies with great care. I found it extremely telling that, the victims were re-dressed after their murders. They were naked when they were killed, yet there was no sign of sexual assault or abuse. He is treating the victims with a kind of bizarre respect. In effect thanking them for their lives."

"Human sacrifices? Like the Aztecs? Treated like royalty prior to being killed?" I asked, trying to be sure I had the full picture.

"Not exactly, Mike. I don't know that they were treated par-ticularly well. But, except for New Mexico and the retired cop in Connecticut, there was no real sign of struggle. They were either willing victims, which I think is extremely unlikely, or they were sufficiently intimidated to submit."

"Or drugged," I offered.

"Yes. Or drugged. In that sense, they *do* resemble the Aztec sacrifices. Their sacrifices were both intimidated *and* drugged."

"You think the killer believes he is benefiting from the deaths of his victims." It was a statement.

"Yes, not to mention the wounds on the victims' hands."

"What about them?"

"These are the places that the American Indians used to draw blood for blood oaths. Many pagan cults do the same. That is a part of the body that bleeds easily even from modest incisions. It just bolsters my theory about ceremony and/or sacrifice."

"Okay. You keep saying 'he.' Definitely a male?" I thought I knew what she would say.

"Yes. There's no sex angle, but the communications you've found on the bodies strongly suggests a male. There appears to be at least an undertone of sexual motivation. Not to mention that a considerable amount of physical strength would be required to move the bodies."

"My thoughts exactly. What else?"

"I'd also say this killer is a classic serial-killer personality in the following respects: he's organized, apparently charming or handsome, or both. He's got some social skills, most likely well educated, intelligent, articulate."

"Sounds like me."

"Hardly. This person is an off-the-rack, king-hell sociopath. A person that, despite his charms, has no regard for human life whatsoever. In effect, he sees other people as objects or tools to be used in gaining some objective."

"Wouldn't the sacrifices themselves be the objective?"

"No. They'd be the *motivation*." She replied.

"In other words, we need to ask what is he sacrificing these victims *for?*"

"Precisely."

"So let's talk that through for a minute, Jacquie. What was the purpose of human sacrifice in ancient cultures? To correct some perceived misfortune in their society, right? Like a bad harvest, or bad weather, right?"

"Right."

"People were ritually killed to appease the gods," I went on. "To give them their expected ration of blood. Sometimes it was in exchange for some gift to be bestowed by the deities, like good luck or immortality. Isn't that pretty much it?"

"Those are the biggies," she answered.

"Do you think that our guy is motivated differently?"

"I'm just not certain..." The words fell into the room followed by a short, uncomfortable wordlessness. "You're probably right, Mike. I don't know why I'm fighting that."

"Let me run something by you," I said. "I've got a theory, but I want to hear your thoughts. What do you make of the absence of a show of force prior to what I'll call the 'killing blow.' The knife to the heart? It's as though the killer is using an almost humane method of dispatching his victims once he's gotten what he wants from them."

She was silent a few moments. "The killer had to gain the confidence of the victims. He had to get close, engage them in conversation, charm them into leaving wherever he had initially met them, so that he could commence his ritual and ultimately kill them. I'd have to conclude that he is poised enough to initiate contact; attractive or safe-looking enough to gain their trust; articulate enough to charm them into leaving; organized enough to carry out his ritual; and strong enough to move the bodies to where they were ultimately found."

"I've been thinking," I said slowly, "we're looking for a man in his mid-twenties to early-thirties. But my money is on the younger end of the spectrum."

"Why?"

"Two reasons. The younger victims might have been frightened or intimidated by the approach of a man significantly older than they. And as for the older victims: they would be flattered to gain the attention of a handsome younger man."

"What about the men? There was no gay angle," she asked.

"Again, a younger, honest-looking man would not be intimidating to a military man. As for the cop in Connecticut, he was caught in a home invasion. He had no choice. He had been *selected*."

"Same for the 911 dispatcher," she put in.

"Exactly."

"What about that?" Jacquie tested me.

"I think the victims have been chosen to fulfill something specific for the killer. Most of the victims' careers are fairly well identifiable. A military man — in uniform, no less. A stripper. A call girl. A flight attendant. All of these would be almost immediately recognizable as doing what they do for a living. Less so the students, but I don't think it's coincidence that they were both UCLA coeds."

"Meaning?"

"That the victims themselves are part of the message."

"I believe you're dead-on, Mike. And one other thing: so is the geography. In fact, I think the geography may be even more important to the killer than the victims' professions."

It felt like an electric shock. "What?" Something stirring in my subconscious.

"The places these victims were found are important to the killer."

"You mean a parking lot, or the Hollywood Bowl."

"I think so, Mike. But be careful not to be too literal, too specific. I mean, don't lose sight of the states, counties or cities where these crimes have been committed. I'd stay general on that."

"What about the killer's race?" I asked.

"Caucasian," she answered without hesitation.

"I agree." Statistics bear out that a non-Caucasian serial killer is a rare bird. But more importantly, the fact that the killer had to be able to casually approach his victims without being noticeable or the slightest bit unusual. He'd need to blend in to the scenery in every locale that the victims' bodies had been discovered. A white male would still find it easier to do that.

"What about the 'messages' found with the bodies? What's that about?"

"You may not like this, Mike, but I don't think they're

meant for you. I think they're part of the ritual."

"Go on."

"In other words, they mean much more to the killer, and possibly the victim, than to you or me. This is not, in my opinion, some unspoken desire to be caught by the authorities like so many of these kinds of messages are. It doesn't strike me that they are designed to taunt. I think it's more like an explanation than a road sign."

I started to ask my next question.

"Mike, I'm sorry to interrupt, but I'm almost out of time before my first appointment. You got most of the important stuff already anyway. In another day or so, I'll have all this written up so you can circulate it among the team. In the meantime, I hope what I've told you is useful."

"It's great, Jacquie, and I really appreciate it. By the way, I'm going to be asked about your fee."

"I'll bill you. It won't be much. The department can afford it."

"Thanks again —"

She cut me off. "There is one other thing you can do, though."

"What's that?"

"Take me out to a nice dinner some time. Avalon, maybe...." Her voice blanketed the room as if she were there with me.

"I thought you were married, Jacquie."

"I was. But not anymore. A lot happens in a year and a half. You've got to keep up."

"And here I thought you shrinks had it all figured out. In touch with your emotions and all that."

She laughed a husky, sexy laugh. "I'll look forward to dinner."

"Me too," I said, and hung up.

Our voices seemed to echo in the room. A hotel is a lonely place.

*   *   *

I FINISHED dressing and gathered up the files I had strewn about the room. As I tucked the folders under my arm, I felt as much as heard the vibration of my ringing cell-phone.

"I hope I'm not calling too early," Deana said.

"I was just heading out the door."

"Then I'm glad I caught you. I *had* to call you, Mike." She sounded breathless. "I took your advice."

I didn't remember giving her any. "Uh huh."

"I decided to get in touch with my real family. I mean, I thought and thought about what you said to me at dinner the other night, and you were right. So I did it. I called my mom and she was able to track down my birth mother."

"How'd she do that?" I asked.

"Through the doctor that originally arranged the adoption. It's a long story, but the man knew where to find her. I mean, where my birth mother could be reached."

"That's great, Deana."

"Not really. When I called the number my mom gave me, someone else answered. She told me that the woman I was looking for had been very ill. She's in a coma as we speak. She's not expected to live." Deana's voice sounded brittle.

"Jesus, Deana. I'm sorry."

A heavy silence hung between us, then she cleared her throat. "There's more, Mike," she hesitated. "She has another child."

"Your birth mother?"

"Yeah, can you believe it? I've got a sibling out there I didn't even know about. Isn't that cool?"

"But I need your help, Mike. I have his name, but no number. The person who answered the phone didn't have it. She couldn't even tell me what *city* to look in. You can get a phone number from just a name, right? I mean the police have ways of doing that, don't they?"

She sounded anxious, agitated.

"Sure. It might take a little while." I glanced at my watch. "And I've got a meeting downtown in —"

She interrupted, "I know you're busy, but I really need your help. It probably sounds stupid Mike, but all of a sudden it seems so much more important now that I know she's dying.... I really want to do this."

"I understand. Let me get a pen."

I dropped my files on the bed and wrote the name she gave me on a sheet of hotel message paper, and slipped it in my pocket. I would call my phone-company contact on the way downtown. What was the use of strings if you couldn't pull a few for a friend.

"I'll call you back when I have a number for you."

"You're the best. Call me back at Pete's, okay?"

I told her I would, gathered my files and went down to get in my crappy little car. The damn thing was giving me a gun-butt bruise over my kidney.

Chapter Fourteen

"YOU OWE ME BIG, TRAVIS," VONDA FRANKLIN said as I arrived at her cubicle. "It took me 'til one o'clock this morning."

"Tell me what we got."

"It's a car, all right. All that shows is the front tire and hubcap, front bumper, front left fender and..." she teased. A few hours sleep had brought back her bounce.

"*What?*"

"A partial plate."

"You gotta be shitting me." It was better than I had hoped. "How partial?"

"I shit you not. We got the first three numbers. Totally legible."

Now all I had to hope for was that the car belonged to the killer, not just some junkie going down to the pier to score dope in the middle of the night. Junkies made horrible witnesses.

"You said 'numbers.' California plates have a different

sequence. One number, three letters, three more numbers."

"It's a California plate, all right. Just a real old one. Three numbers, three letters." She dug out one of the still photos she had made. "Look here. You can see the first few letters of the word 'California' right there at the top. See? C - A - L - I. Plain as day."

The numbers read 8 - 9 - 7.

"One other thing," she added. "I showed the pictures to a couple of the guys down here. They're both pretty sure that the car is a 1970 or '71 Volkswagen van. They said you can tell by the bumper here."

"Any guesses about the color?"

"Based on the gray-scale, I'd say the bottom half is that pukey green color they used to have, really faded red, or yellow. The top is definitely white. That funky two-tone shit they were using back then."

I reached for the photos.

She pulled them out of my reach. "Now say it again."

"My yacht. Clear water and sunshine..."

"God, yes," she said, and handed me the photos and video.

*   *   *

I MADE a bee line for the Homicide division.

When I arrived, Hans was on the phone. He held up five fingers as he saw me walk in. I sat at an unoccupied desk, thumbed through Vonda's photos, and waited the five minutes for him to finish.

"What you got, Travis?"

"News. I've got news."

"Me, too," he said in return. "I go first."

I held up both hands, palms up.

"Kemp ran down the phone number. There were a hundred possible combinations, right? Well, the prefixes that cover Westwood had only three numbers that would have fit the missing space that were active exchanges. Five-two-*zero* and five-two-*two*."

"So that brought the possibilities down to only thirty," I put in.

"Right. Now, since we already had three of the last four numbers in the sequence, it was just a matter of smilin' and dialin'."

"Kemp? Smilin' and dialin'?"

"Give it a rest, Travis. Anyway, he made his calls, he found only six of the thirty possibilities were active numbers."

"Yeah?"

"The others hadn't been given out yet. They had all been disconnected within the last six months, so they hadn't been reassigned yet."

"He called all six? Did he speak to everybody?"

"Sure enough. But there was only one that wasn't ruled out after talking to the occupant. Anyway, that was the phone company on the line just now. We got the address for the one we like. So we got a lead," Hans finished, visibly pleased.

"Nice work. But if you like that sorry little thing, you're gonna love this bit of detective work. Ready?"

"Dazzle me."

"I got a usable photo off the People's Bank of Venice ATM video. It shows a vehicle parked for a short period of time, right where he should have been if he wanted to dump a body, and within the proper time frames to have been the guy. How about that shit?"

Broad smile.

"But wait, there's more," I gloated. "I've got a partial plate, too. And it gets even better: it's a not-too-common model that we might even be able to track down through DMV." I dropped the photos on his desk.

"Volkswagen?" he observed.

"VW van. I'm told it's probably 1970 or 1971. Two-tone. White over monkey-barf green, faded red or yellow."

"Let's put it through Motor Vehicles. If there aren't a thousand cars that meet these specs, we might just have something." He looked up from the glossies. "You know, Mike, if we're not careful, we might just get a break on this case."

"We could damn well use one."

"Townsend!" Hans hollered over the everyday din of ringing telephones and typewriters. The young detective hurried over. Hans gave him what we had of the license plate and the possible color combinations of the suspect car. "Get that to DMV and have them fax whatever they find ASAP. And tell the PA to notify me when it arrives."

"I spoke with Jacquie Whitney this morning and we worked out a thumbnail sketch of the killer. She's going to write it up and get it to us in the next couple of days. I was going to run it down for everyone tomorrow. No sense going over it twice."

"Anything you hadn't thought of before?"

"Yeah. There's some interesting stuff on the guy's motivation. We talked it out and it sounds plausible. There's a ritual element to it we hadn't considered. She thinks the location of the body dumps is a key. There're a couple of other things, but I need to sleep on them myself before I can endorse them."

"So what's your plan for the day?" Hans asked.

"I need a copy of the New Orleans file to review before tomorrow. But you're the boss. You're the one that called me over."

"I've got Bobb and Townsend covering the Courson funeral today. Place will be crawling with photographers and cops, so I don't need you there."

"You think the guy will show?" It was not uncommon for a killer to go to a victim's funeral. Hans was hoping that if the guy we were hunting showed up, we'd catch his face on film. We would later compare crowd photos from the prior L.A. victims' funerals with those from Patti Courson's and see if anyone showed up at more than just one.

"No," Hans answered bluntly. "Why don't you come with me and Kemp to interview the phone guy."

"Let's do it."

Hans nodded and shrugged himself into a dark blue sportcoat, adjusting it as it snagged on the handle of the SIG-Sauer 9mm that was secured in his shoulder holster.

*   *   *

HANS SAT behind the wheel of the unmarked car, studying the road as he drove. I knew he was mentally rehearsing the questions he was preparing to ask Mr. Robert Fornier, occupant of the apartment whose telephone number had been found on Patti Courson's desk calendar. Dan Kemp sat beside him. I sat in back.

"You okay driving, Hans," Kemp asked.

"Fine."

"I can spell you if you want."

"I said I'm fine."

"Whatsamatter, Hans, didn't get laid last night?"

What Kemp got in return was a brief, hard stare, the muscles in Hans' jaw working tightly.

"Now, I on the other hand, had quite a successful night," Kemp went on unfazed by Hans' obvious unwillingness to engage in conversation.

Hans shot me a look in the rearview mirror as his knuckles whitened on the steering wheel.

"Yessirree, you remember that blonde-haired teller on the Merchant's Bank case?"

Kemp was referring to a case in which a man had entered a bank, intending to rob it, only to find an old high-school acquaintance behind the counter, employed there as a teller. The irony was that the man had driven over one hundred and fifty miles to rob this particular bank, assuming that he would not be recognized by anyone so distant from where he lived. The robber panicked when he recognizing the blonde, and made all seven people in the bank lie face down on the floor. The thief had then proceeded to summarily fire a bullet into the base of each person's skull.

When he reached his fourth intended victim, the blonde from high-school, his gun jammed. In a fit of panic, the robber dropped the weapon and ran. But the entire act had been caught on tape.

The teller, an average-looking blonde named Nicole Wright, later testified as an eyewitness in court. The shooter was serving out three consecutive life sentences.

Hans and I said nothing, hoping that Kemp would stop talking.

"Yeah, well, there I was, standing buck-ass naked —"

"Aw, shit, Kemp. Now I gotta picture you naked?

"You don't want to hear my fuck story?"

"No. I *especially* don't want to hear *your* fuck story."

Kemp shrugged, looked out the passenger side window.

I suppressed a desire to laugh out loud.

My phone rang. It was Trina Foley, my contact at the phone company.

"I've got the number you wanted. I gotta tell you it wasn't easy. It's a cell phone, and it was a bitch finding it. But it's the only listing with the name you gave me."

I pulled the folded piece of hotel paper from my pocket and readied my pen. "Thanks for the effort, Trina. Fire away," I said and she rattled off a number.

"Got the address?" I asked.

"You didn't tell me you wanted an address, Mike."

"Did."

"Didn't."

We had dated briefly. I hadn't done a very good job of saying goodbye, and an even worse job of remaining in touch since I had left L.A. She was making me pay.

"Will you get it for me anyway?" I asked politely.

"It'll be the billing address. Will that do?"

"As long as it's a real address, not a PO box." I replied.

"It'll be a street address. Company policy."

"Great."

"I'll get back to you later," she said after a slight pause.

"I'd appreciate it if you would."

"Good to hear you squirm, Mike."

"Okay, you've made your point. I'm sorry I haven't kept in touch," I said. Hans caught my eye in the rearview again and raised his eyebrows mockingly.

"Fair enough. It's just lucky for you I'm such a pushover for handsome sailors." She snickered and rang off.

"Professional call?" Hans needled.

Five long minutes later we pulled to the curb in front of a

four-story apartment building just outside of Westwood. Kemp consulted his open notebook and double checked the address.

"Number three-oh-three. Wanna buzz the manager first?" Kemp asked, pointing to the rows of black buttons positioned beneath an assortment of presstape name labels.

"Naw, let's just go on up. Security gate's open," Hans paused momentarily and looked at Kemp. "Now listen, this could be our guy, so keep cool, all right?"

He said nothing. I could see his resentment at Yamaguchi's talking him through the procedure as if he were a rookie. I reckoned Kemp would have a talk with the lieutenant about that when we got back.

We entered the gateway that guarded a narrow set of worn linoleum stairs ascending to an elevator lobby about half a floor up. The only light in the stairwell came from a pair of dim sconces on either side of the elevator door above. The daylight cast long shadows. Our silhouettes zigzagged up before us.

We bypassed the elevator, and took the stairs to the upper floors marked with an illuminated "Exit" sign. Taking the steps two at a time, my heartbeat accelerated with the adrenaline that pumped through my veins. It had been awhile.

Not knowing whether the person behind the door of apartment 303 was a psychopathic killer, or merely a friend of the most recent victim, kept me focused. Totally there. Like slow motion.

Hans signaled for Kemp and me to stand to one side of the door frame. Hans stood opposite. No one stood directly in front of the paint peeling door. We each drew our weapons, barrels pointing at the ceiling. I tensed as Yamaguchi reached over and rapped hard on the door.

"Yeah. Just a minute," came from inside the apartment. The

sound of approaching footsteps from the other side of the door was followed by the scrape of metallic bolts, and the rattle of a security chain. The door opened.

"Yeah? *Shit!*" The young man's voice went from mildly irritated at having been interrupted to abject fear when he saw all the guns.

"Police detectives," Hans announced. "Are you Robert Fornier?"

"Y- yeah. What *is* this?" Robert stammered. He was tall and gawky, dressed in loose chinos and a button down shirt.

"May we come in?" Hans pressed, not answering his question.

"Yeah... I guess... sure." A prominent adam's apple bobbed up and down.

Kemp and I crossed the threshold quickly, and Hans motioned for Kemp to look through the one-bedroom apartment. Moments later, he returned to the small living room confirming that no one else was there.

"Sorry we scared you," I said to Fornier as I holstered my gun.

"I could have told you —"

"I just apologized, okay?" I interrupted.

His face reddened.

"Live here alone, Mr. Fornier? Mind if I call you Bob?" Hans asked.

"No. I mean, yes. I mean, 'yes' I live here alone, and 'no' I don't mind if you call me Bob." A worn text book was propped open on the table. Fornier's hands trembled as they hung loosely at his sides.

"Mind if we all sit down?" Kemp asked, gesturing with his thumb toward the sofa behind where he stood.

"No. That's fine," he answered, leading the way.

"Nice poster," Kemp said. "You don't look old enough to know Janis Joplin."

Fornier looked at his feet, shrugged.

"Bob, we want to ask you a few questions, okay?" Hans said, as he withdrew the miniature tape recorder from his jacket pocket and placed it on the table, the small red light glowing.

"Sure," the young man said, glancing nervously at the recorder.

"Do you know Patti Courson?"

"Patti *who?*"

"Courson, Bob," Kemp put in.

"No. I've never heard of her. Why?"

"We're investigating a murder. She was the victim. Are you certain you don't know her?" Hans said.

"Yeah, I'm positive."

"Then how would you explain that your phone number was found in her apartment? Or why the victim's phone records show that she placed a call to your number?" I prodded. The bad cop.

"I have no... wait a minute... When was this? This *murder?*" He said the word as if it left a foul taste in his mouth. As it should.

"Over the weekend. Can you tell me where you were last Friday and Saturday, Bob?" I asked, leaning closer, invading his space, beginning to intimidate him.

"Yeah. The same place I was the weekend before that. San Jose. Actually, Santa Cruz. Visiting my parents. They just moved up there."

"You've got proof you could show me?" Hans' eyebrows arched.

"Plane tickets? I'll get them if you want to see 'em."

"Yeah, Bob, we would. Why don't you go get them," Kemp said.

Robert Fornier left the room momentarily, followed casually by Kemp, and returning with a dog-eared American Airlines ticket jacket. He handed it to Hans, who looked it over, then passed it to me. The tickets had been issued in Fornier's name, and indicated he'd been gone over the weekend, just as he had said, having returned only the day before. I passed them back to Kemp.

"You were there the entire time?" Hans asked.

"Yes. You can call my parents. I'll give you their number," he volunteered hastily.

"I'll do that. How about you write down their number?"

The young man scratched something on a piece of spiral-bound notebook, tore it out, and started to hand it to me.

"Give it to Detective Kemp," I said.

Kemp took it and strode to a phone on the kitchen counter. We didn't want to give anyone time to concoct stories.

"You said you live alone?" Hans repeated.

"Uh... yeah."

"And you don't know anyone named Patricia Courson? Is that right?"

"Yeah. That's right." Indignant now. Getting his balls back.

"So why would someone you don't even know call your apartment, I wonder?" I asked. "Was there somebody else here while you were gone?"

"Well...uh... yeah," he stammered nervously, eyes darting, unable to remain focused on any one object for long. He could hear Kemp speaking softly on the kitchen phone.

"You seem uncomfortable all of a sudden, Bob," I said.

"Listen..." he started, looking quickly from Hans' face to mine. "I'm just a student here, okay? I don't know anyone named Carlson or whatever you said. And I don't know anything about any *murder* for God's sake."

"Uh huh," Hans said, priming the pump.

"I let a friend use the apartment while I was away. That's *all*. He's a guy I know from back in high school, okay? He wanted to hang out in L.A. for a few days. Needed a place to crash. Maybe he partied a little or something, but, shit, he's no *killer*."

"What's this friend's name?" I asked.

"Why do you need to know that?"

"Well, *Bob*, as I explained a few minutes ago, we're investigating a *murder* here. Now that might not mean much to *you*, but it *is* kind of important to *us*."

The young man's face began to flush again. He didn't like me much.

"So," I continued, "because we get in trouble if we don't catch the people who *kill* other people when they aren't supposed to, we end up having to talk to all kinds of assholes. In this case, that now includes both *you* and your *friend*. So how about telling us about what went on here while you were away at Mommy and Daddy's, *okay?*"

*   *   *

WE WERE on the 405 freeway heading south, toward Long Beach. Hans was edging over toward the carpool lane and Kemp was searching a Thomas Brothers map book for the address we had been given for Bob Fornier's friend, Don Kazem. I dialed the number for Pete's Roadhouse from memory.

Far off to my left, as the phone began to ring in my ear, I watched a thick layer of gray clouds gather over the coastline.

"Pete's," a voice yelled into my ear, laughter, rock music and clanking glasses providing the background. I had a sudden urge for beer.

"Hey, Boss, this is Mike," I said, smiling at the mental picture I held of the place.

"Hey, Pete! It's Travis on the phone," the voice hollered, not too close to the receiver. "This's Singin' Dude, Travis," the voice said to me this time. "Where you been?"

"On the mainland. L.A.," I answered. "Sorry to miss your dance the other night. Your headache clear up yet?"

"Ooooh, man. That was a real bad judgment call on my part. That's about as hung over as you can get without dying. Fuck me, man, my dancing days are through," he laughed.

"Sounds like a song," I said, and riffed an imitation of Led Zeppelin's *Dancing Days*. I ignored Kemp's look.

"Funny guy, Travis. Anyway, buddy, here's Pete."

A moment later, Pete's voice came on the line. "Hey 'ya, Mike."

"Hey, Boss. Nothing personal, but I was actually calling for Deana. She's there, isn't she?"

"Ain't she always?"

"Mind if I talk to her for a sec?"

"Sure. When you getting back to the island? I've got about three cases of that Jap beer you drink and nobody else will touch it."

"Good damn thing, too," I said.

I heard Pete chuckle, put the phone down and call for Deana. A full minute passed, and I watched the cloud cover grow thicker over the coastline.

"Hey," Deana said.

"Hey, yourself. It sounds busy there, so I'll make this quick. I got that number you wanted." I read it to her. "But I'll have to call you later with the address."

"I don't know how to thank you, Mike. That was really nice. I'm going to use it right away."

"Don't mention it."

"When are you coming back?"

"Hard to say. I don't know."

"Well, I hope it's soon. Thanks again, Mike. Really."

Sometimes you're the windshield, sometimes you're the bug.

Chapter Fifteen

*I*N THE ANCIENT TIMES THEY USED TO DANCE *naked in the forests.*

"We are the protectors of the Seasons," the Cicerone had taught him.

And he would respond, "We are Destroyers."

The time of the original Mysteries fascinated him. In those days thousands of years ago, bands of women roamed the hills of the old country. Feral women, looting, fucking, eating animals raw. Coming upon unsuspecting victims and tearing them to pieces. Seeking deep truths about life beyond the grave. Looking for Dionysius.

Chapter Sixteen

Hans navigated the odd conglomeration of modern avenues and narrow streets with their cracked and crudely patched pavement. Primarily a working port, Long Beach was attempting to redefine itself as a convention and tourist destination with attractions such as the Queen Mary and Howard Hughes' enormous seaplane, the Spruce Goose. The outcome thus far was mixed.

Small portions of the city had been somewhat improved, if you counted the construction of a couple of hotels and green-belts as improvement. The remainder had been left to continue their steady decline, a latticework of avenues bordered by aging and tawdry buildings.

A Mom and Pop grocery off to my right caught my attention and activated my subconscious, taking me back to a call-out I had rolled on years before, when I was still a first-year cherry in a radio unit.

Mine had been the first patrol unit to arrive, and I could still remember the bile that rose in my throat as I entered the store and found the elderly Korean male, the owner, lying on his side behind the counter, thick blood pooling beneath his balding head. A twenty-five-cent ball-point pen was protruding from his ear, where it had been placed and then stomped into his brain cavity by a boot. The cash register drawer was still open and empty, jutting out from the machine, casting a shadow across the dead man's face.

His wife had been raped, beaten and left for dead in the storeroom in the back. Between the commission of the crimes and my unit's arrival on the scene, looters had invaded the store and stripped the shelves and floor displays. All while the owners, long-time residents and business owners in the neighborhood, lay on the floor bleeding and dying.

After awakening from the coma induced by the trauma of the beating she took, the old woman was able to identify the two assholes who had invaded their little business from a photographic lineup. The district attorney, a gutless rodent named Vic Moss, refused to prosecute on the basis that, despite the ID of the perps by the lone remaining living victim, the looters had left too many fingerprints behind to enable him to successfully tie the killers to the crime.

Some time later, I had watched my then-partner, Reginald Carter, a twenty-plus veteran of the streets, dress down the bookish A.D.A., punctuating every point he made with regard to the attorney's absence of balls, integrity, and morality with the jab of a stiff forefinger to his bony chest. Each nudge propelled the wimpy barrister backwards, his eyes growing wider and wider with each of Reggie Carter's shoves. Moss was still with the D.A.'s office.

That had been my first glimpse into the system.

A loud, wet splat emanated from the windshield and woke me from my preoccupation with crime and punishment. A white dollop of seagull shit slid slowly down the glass. Hans activated the wiper, and proceeded to liberally distribute it in a broad arc across the driver's side of the windshield. He pulled on a lever beside the steering wheel, but nothing happened.

"God damn it. No wiper fluid."

A little birdshit rainbow.

The house we were looking for was in a neighborhood of seemingly random single-story square stucco boxes that had probably languished on the edge of acceptability in the early 1970's. It had since yielded to taggers and street punks who spray-painted or boosted anything that stood still for too long.

We finally found the address we were looking for. The house was sandwiched between a garbage-strewn, weed-strangled lot and a faded yellow clapboard house with iron bars over the windows.

The neighbor's front yard looked like an auto graveyard. The centerpiece was a late-1960's pickup truck propped on cinder blocks, stripped of all four wheels, hood, and the passenger side door. Two more empty carcasses sat at odd angles around the pickup, resting on rust-streaked concrete blocks.

Graffiti defaced all three vehicles. A snaking curlicue of black spray paint ended in an arrowhead that pointed to a bullet hole that had spider-webbed the truck's windshield.

"What a fucking sty," I said.

"Okay, boys. Let's do it again," Hans sighed and drew his pistol.

"If the prick hasn't split already," Kemp put in. "Whattaya bet Fornier called him and told him we're coming?"

"I don't know," I laughed. "When I told him not to, he looked like he was going to piss his pants."

* * *

IT WAS nearly five p.m. by the time we got back to Homicide. The end of the shift was coming up, and everyone on the floor seemed busy tying things up before taking off for the night. Loo was on the phone when Hans knocked and asked if we could see him. Loo gestured to the chairs in front of his desk, and Hans, Kemp and I went in and waited for him to hang up.

"We've had some interesting developments today," Hans began.

"Your interview with the telephone number guy?" Loo confirmed.

"Yeah. Turns out he's a real pencil-neck who wasn't even there when the call was made to his place. Tells us he let an old high-school buddy use his apartment while he was gone to his parents in northern California. So we press the guy, and he finally gives us this high-school friend's name — a guy who lives down in Long Beach.."

Loo waited. Patient. One of the things that made him so good at what he did.

"So we shag ass down to Stanton," Hans went on. "Only to find *another* pencil-neck. But this one — his name is Don Kazem — claims he wasnsn't at the apartment either. I call bullshit on that, right?

"Well, the guy starts getting nervous all of a sudden, and wants to know whether we have to tell his friend Bob Fornier that he — this Kazem guy — had let *another* friend use the apartment instead."

"Fornier tells his buddy Don that he can use his place while he's out of town, only instead of Don using the place himself, he lets a *third* guy use it," Kemp clarified.

"Exactly," Hans nods.

Loo got up and closed the mini-blinds that covered the glass walls of his office. He reached into his desk drawer and pulled out a pack of cigarettes.

"No gum?" I said.

"It's the end of the shift, Travis. You gonna bust my balls?"

I raised my hands in surrender.

The lieutenant flipped open a Marine Corps zippo and fired up his smoke.

"And...?"

"Well, Don's all nervous all of a sudden," Hans continued. "Starts squirming and wanting a lawyer and shit. I tell him we're just running down some leads on a case and there's no need to get defensive, right? Of course, I'm thinking 'This is the fucking guy. This is the killer.' But, no."

Loo sighed. He exhaled a blue cloud and Hans went on.

"Now *this* asshole comes across with an alibi, but he doesn't want anybody else to know. Seems he was doing somebody and something that he wasn't supposed to be doing."

Loo smiled and drew deep on his cigarette.

It was often like that. Somebody cheating where he wasn't supposed to be, then has to cop to it in order to keep from getting hung for something even worse. Wrong place at the wrong time. Bad karma.

"To make a long story short —" Hans said.

"— Too late," Loo said.

"We get the name of the bimbo he was with, and confirm his story. It's his girlfriend's best friend, it turns out. What a dumbass.

"Anyway, so the guy's alibi is clean, but Mike starts leaning on him about obstructing the investigation of a murder case, and being an accessory after the fact and all this other shit, to get the guy to give up the name of the asshole who *was* at the apartment when Patti Courson called."

Loo leaned forward.

"Well, Don finally admits that he's all shook up about telling us the name of the guy who used the place because he's afraid of the guy. Doesn't even know his name. Turns out that old Donny boy buys weed from this other guy and doesn't want any of this murder shit to come back on him in the form of some narcotics bust or something."

"He *volunteered* all of this? About the grass? Out of the blue?" Loo asked incredulously, though we had all seen plenty of strange things happen during interviews.

"Yeah, can you believe it? I mean it's not like we were there busting his chops about drugs or anything. Hell, it hadn't even come up, but the guy just blurts it out."

Hans looked at me. "You tell the rest."

"I asked for the address where this dealer lives and Don says he doesn't know. I called bullshit, but Don says, no, he really doesn't know, but he can show us. I say, sure. Let's go ahead and take a ride and you can show me the guy's house."

Hans couldn't resist, and jumped in. " 'Right now?' Don asks. 'Yeah, right fucking now,' Travis tells him. 'Don't make me tell you all about obstruction of justice again,' he says. That shut old Don right up and he turns into Mr. Cooperative again."

"So then what happened?" Loo asked quizzically. Hans was not normally given to long, detailed stories like the one he was recounting.

"So we get in the car and take a ride all the way down to the beach. We get to a trailer park near Pacific Coast Highway in Huntington Beach, and Don says this is the place. 'Which one?' I ask, and he gets nervous all over again. He says he doesn't want anybody seeing him with us. After I reminded him how little I gave a shit about who saw him with us, he directed us to this one specific trailer in the park."

"These are like little trailers? Travel trailers?" Loo inquired.

"No. Like the kind old people live in. Why?"

"No reason. I'm just trying to follow the details is all," he answered.

"So we knock, and nobody answers. Don's been with us the entire time, so I know he didn't tip him, but regardless, we're stuck."

"You get a statement from this Don character?" Loo asked, crushing out his cigarette.

"Handwritten and signed," Kemp said.

"Then let's put in for a warrant on the trailer." The lieutenant stashed the ashtray in a desk drawer and looked at his watch. "It probably won't be issued until tomorrow."

"No problem. We got the team meeting first thing, anyway," Hans said.

Loo opened the mini-blinds, then picked up a fax from his desktop. "This came to me by mistake. It's your DMV printout on the van."

Hans took it and handed it to Kemp to follow up.

The three of us began to file out of the hot and smoky office, when I felt a hand on my shoulder. I turned.

"How did it feel today?" the lieutenant asked me.

A million thoughts rushed through my head. "Good, Loo," I answered finally. "Damn good."

Chapter Seventeen

W̶E SPENT THE NEXT THREE HOURS GOING OVER the new information that had come in while we were out. Kemp took the DMV printouts, Hans discussed the Courson funeral with Bobb and Townsend, while I read the autopsy report on the dead girl from the Whisky.

Her name was Felicia Vanson, age twenty-four, a book-keeper at a carpet showroom over on Robertson, not far from the club where she had been found. The narrative confirmed what we had suspected as the cause of death: a single penetration of the heart with a dual-edged blade. The words on the victim's inner thighs were thought to have been carved pre-mortem with a razor. Traces of adhesive consistent with duct tape were found on her wrists, ankles and face. She had been gagged to muffle her screaming as the killer carved his message. The autopsy had also revealed soap particles all over the body, from neck to the bottoms of the victim's feet.

Jacquie is right, I thought to myself. *The guy treats the bodies with unusual care.*

Primary and secondary blood toxicology showed fairly substantial alcohol levels, but also a heavy concentration of D-Lysergic Acid Diethylamide. LSD.

I looked up from the report. "Hey, Hans. Did the secondary blood-tox report come back on Patti Courson?"

He shuffled through a pile of papers in his in-box. "Yeah. Here it is," he answered. He pushed the folder to me across the smooth linoleum floor.

"Thanks." I scanned it until I found what I was looking for. "Get this," I said. "Both Patti Courson and Felicia Vanson had high concentrations of alcohol and LSD in their systems at the time of death. That strike you as odd?"

Hans was pensive a moment. "Yeah, it does. Remember what Courson's roommate said? Acid is a pretty heavy-duty hallucinogen for a straight-shooter like Patti was supposed to be."

"That's what I'm thinking. What do we know about Vanson?"

Hans looked over at Bobb. He and Townsend had done the interviews with co-workers and neighbors.

"She lived alone over off Sunset," he began. "Owner of the store where she worked said she was reliable, hard worker, no family problems that he knew of."

"Partied sometimes with friends," Townsend added. "Club-hopping, dancing, like that. Nobody said anything about drugs."

"Your average working girl, then?" I asked.

"That's the picture we got," Bobb answered as he shot a glance at Townsend. Townsend nodded.

"I don't remember LSD showing up in the tox screens on any of the other victims," I commented.

Hans looked over. "I don't think any of the other screens went beyond level one. I don't think Sharon would have done a secondary on either Courson *or* Vanson if we hadn't asked."

I shook my head. "You're probably right. Too late to find out now." It pissed me off that we might have missed an opportunity to identify another unusual aspect of these killings.

By the time I finished reading the report in its entirety and the case file that had been sent over from New Orleans, my eyes were red and dry. I felt puny from the poor night's sleep I had the night before, on top of which, the next morning's team meeting had been moved up to seven o'clock so that we could roll right away when the search warrant on the drug dealer's trailer came through.

The office was unusually quiet, and I could hear the buzzing of the fluorescent lights over the muted sounds of traffic outside.

"I'm gonna call it a night," I announced. Hans said he was, too. Bobb, Townsend and Kemp had left an hour earlier. "See you in the morning, then."

"Yeah. Get some sleep. You look like hell."

"Thanks. You, too."

*　　　*　　　*

I RODE the elevator from the underground parking garage to the hotel lobby. As the doors opened, I was greeted by the noise of several dozen drunken businessmen scattered about the lobby bar in tight groups. Boozy eyes shone wetly from pink and mottled faces. Overhead lights reflected off bald pates.

Cigar smoke trailed from waving hands. A convention. Wonderful.

I stopped by the newsstand to pick up a paper. I hadn't read one since I had re-joined the team, and I wanted to see what they were saying about our cases.

I was examining the wooden rack that displayed magazines, paperback books and papers for a copy of the *Times*. I grabbed a copy from a small stack and went to the counter.

A young woman sat on a stool beside the register reading. She looked up when I approached.

"Room charge?" she asked.

"Yes," I said and gave her my room number and name.

I laid the newspaper on the counter. "I'd like one of those Macanudo cigars there behind you," I said. I was going to give it to Loo and tell him that if he was going to bother to break the no smoking policy in the office, he might as well do it right.

She put the magazine she was reading on the counter as she rang up the sale.

I looked absently at the cover as she scanned my purchase. Then something caught my eye. It was the July issue of *Rolling Stone*.

I felt an icy stone in the pit of my stomach.

On the cover was the headline: Thirty Years After His Death, The Lizard King Still Reigns. Jim Morrison's picture stared out at me.

A pure, cold rush of adrenaline coursed through me and I snatched up the magazine and tossed a ten on the counter. Without waiting for change, I charged to the elevator and punched the button impatiently.

"Hey. Wait..." She said from behind me.

I was reading the article before the doors opened, and by the time I reached my room, a number of random facts that had bubbled in my psyche for years had suddenly made sense.

*   *   *

I TUCKED my Beretta snugly into its holster and pulled my dark blue extra-long windbreaker down to conceal it. I ran, rather than drove, the block or so to Hinano's bar.

A layer of low clouds obscured the stars and sealed an ugly wetness in the air. The clouds glowed orange over downtown, and a pale moon reflected weakly off the ocean. I was sweating beneath my jacket as I stopped before the door of the bar, and waited until I caught my breath.

As I entered, the same woman bartender from before was making a pitcher of frothy drinks for a group of college-aged kids who were noisily playing pool in the back room. Two of them groped each other sloppily as they waited by the bar.

"Be with you in a second, pal," the bartender acknowledged. I nodded.

I looked around the room for my drinking buddy from the other night. The one who knew so much about Jim Morrison. I crunched over broken peanut shells as I walked the length of the bar peering into all the booths, and around the corner into the pool room. Loud music I couldn't identify pummeled the place. Nothing.

"What'll it be?" she asked, drying her hands on her stained white apron.

"I need your help. I'm looking for somebody I met in here the other night." She gave me a look like she had heard that one a million times.

"Yeah, well, if she didn't give you her number then, she

probably didn't want you to have it."

"No, it's not a woman. It's a guy who —"

She rolled her eyes theatrically. "Whether it's a man or woman don't make no difference to me, pal. I still can't help you."

I pulled my ID and a ten-dollar bill from my pocket and laid them on the bar.

Leaning in close to her, I said, "I'm looking for a young guy — I don't know his name — he was sitting right here at the bar a couple of nights ago. Long dark hair, black leather jacket, kind of wired, coked-up. Maybe twenty-five, thirty years old or so, clean shaven. Good looking. He was with a kind of a hippie-looking guy in an army fatigue jacket.."

The fat woman eyed the ten. I couldn't tell if she saw the ID or not. Her hand snaked out and grabbed the bill. "I think I know who you mean. What do you want him for?"

"I need to talk to him. It's important. Where is he?" The guy seemed to know a lot about Morrison. I wanted to know what. And why.

"I don't know, pal. He's come in here a couple of times in the past week or so, that's all. I seen him walking around sometimes, but it's not like I know him or nothin'.."

"Have any idea where he lives? Where he works?"

She shook her head. "Like I said, I don't know the guy. But whenever I seen him, he's always got that leather jacket on."

"How about the other one? The hippie guy?"

Her face remained expressionless as she silently eyed me. I dug into my pants pocket for another bill and tossed it on the bar.

"Same thing," she said in a bored monotone. "I don't know that one either. But when I see him, it's always the same. He comes in, sits with the leather jacket guy, they hassle a little, then he leaves."

"Nothing else?"

"What'd I tell you before? I don't know 'em." Giving me attitude.

I scribbled my number on a napkin and slid it across the bar. "If either of them comes in here, call me right away."

She didn't touch the napkin.

"Okay?" I said, irritably.

"Yeah, yeah. Okay."

I stepped out into the night and strode toward the beach. My mind was hot as I walked the cracked sidewalk that ran beside the crashing ocean. Bonfires glowed brightly and threw red clusters of sparks into the still night air. A trickle of sweat rolled down my back and I felt the weight of the Beretta.

According to the article in *Rolling Stone*, Jim Morrison, the dark and mysterious singer for the Doors, had walked these same sidewalks. Dropped acid and wrote lyrics on the roof of an industrial building not far from where I stood. Attended film school at UCLA. Wrote poetry teeming with images of death, violence and sex. Got arrested a number of times: in New Haven, Miami and New Orleans. Thrown off a plane in Phoenix.

My mind scrolled through the list of victims.

I scanned every face I passed, every dark corner, and every parked car for a glimpse of the men I was looking for. I stopped into every bar and cafe and gave their descriptions. Nothing. I kept walking, scanning. I had to find one or both.

Because I did not believe in coincidence.

And because of the most unsettling thing I read in that magazine. Morrison died on July 3.

That was tomorrow.

Chapter Eighteen

THE FEELING OF FOREBODING DOGGED ME through the night, following me into a restless sleep. I had walked every street and alley for hours and found nothing.

I woke the next morning to the sound of my wake up call, as tired as I had been when I finally went to bed. I shaved, showered and dressed for the meeting that I had about an hour to get to. I wondered if the BOLO we put out last night had yielded anything. Be on the lookout. Every radio car in the city had descriptions of the two men I had seen at Hinano's.

Driving my rental through the slog of morning traffic, I wondered whether the clouds lurking overhead would deliver their sticky summer storm. The outside air was viscous and ugly.

I found a parking stall in the already crowded lot, rushed through the glass doors into Parker Center at precisely seven o'clock, and made it to the Homicide bureau only five minutes late. As it turned out, Dan Kemp had not yet arrived, making him even later than I.

When I entered the room, I was privately amused by the fact that this meeting seemed identical in almost every respect to the one that I had attended a few days earlier. The participants sat in the same seats, the suits they wore looked the same, as did shirts, ties and facial expressions. Another pink box sat open on the scarred veneer conference table, exposing nothing but doughnut crumbs. I tried to remember how early you had to arrive to actually grab a doughnut of your own.

The New Orleans murder victim's photos and the communication from the murderer that had accompanied it had been added to the rolling bulletin boards that surrounded the table. So had Felicia Vanson's. After greeting the team members, I went immediately to the boards and took a look at the new evidence.

Of particular interest to me was the enlargement of another computer- generated animation that had been left on the body of the New Orleans victim. It was another "detail" from the larger, more comprehensive, sketch found with the body of Patti Courson. This one was a close-up, focused on the gaping maw of the green reptile that emerged from the loins of the shackled woman that had appeared in the Courson drawing.

As I took a seat at the conference table, I pondered the significance. Each of the three most recent victims had been found with artistic representations that stemming from the same drawing.

What the hell was it?

Loo walked in. "Travis?"

"Yeah, Loo."

"Let's go into my office a minute."

I followed him across the hall. I entered first, and he closed the door behind us.

"Go ahead, Mike. Sit," he said, and removed a wad of gum from his mouth, tossed it in the trash beside his desk. He was quiet, gathering his thoughts.

I patted my pockets, remembering the cigar I had bought the night before, but something told me this was not a time for levity.

"You used to partner with Reggie Carter, right?" Loo asked.

"Right." Where was this headed?

"I don't know any other way to tell you this, Mike —-"

And I knew. As sure as I've ever known anything, I knew what was coming.

"— Reggie Carter died last night.."

The air in the room closed around me, and I felt a prick of sweat break on the back of my neck.

"Bullshit," I croaked. Reginald Carter had been a model officer, and had taken a sincere interest in me when I was a rookie. Sort of a father figure within my then-new profession, and everybody who knew me knew that.

"I'm sorry, Mike. It's true."

All the noise in the office outside became a pounding in my ears. "What the hell happened?"

"Suicide. A neighbor found him," Loo said. "No note. Nothing. Just took his old duty weapon and pulled the trigger."

My chest felt tight, and breathing came hard.

"Christ...." I couldn't believe that Reggie was gone. That he would eat his gun.

"I'm truly sorry, Mike," Loo said again through the palpable silence. "I just found out this morning. I didn't want to tell you in there. In front of the squad."

I felt hot tears in my eyes, and blinked them back. Swallowed dryly. "Thanks, Lieutenant."

Loo stood and walked to the door. "Take a couple minutes, Mike. Come on back in when you're ready."

When had I seen Reggie last? How long had it been? Why hadn't I taken the time? I sat quietly for another few minutes then followed Loo into the conference room.

All heads turned as I entered. It was clear that everyone had just been told about Reggie.

"Sorry, Mike," Hans said. It was echoed by Townsend and Bobb.

I nodded.

Kemp walked in moments later. In his hand was a paper bag from McDonalds and a cup of coffee imprinted with familiar golden arches. He noisily opened the bag and withdrew the smeared paper wrapping for a breakfast sandwich.

Hans shot him a look.

"What?" Kemp said.

"Travis' old partner, Reggie Carter died last night," Hans said.

"Oh, hey, sorry Mike. I didn't know...."

Hans had known Reggie too, and I could see he was shaken. I made myself a promise to attend Reggie's memorial no matter what. *Shit.* It was a such a pointless ending.

Loo cleared his throat. "All right," Loo began, signaling the beginning of the meeting. "A lot has transpired in the last forty-eight hours. First, let me tell you that we haven't gotten the go-ahead on the warrant yet, but we'll stand by on that."

"Any word on the BOLO?" I asked.

"Nothing yet."

"Son of a bitch."

Loo turned to face Hans. "Yamaguchi? How do you want to proceed on the warrant?"

"I've been thinking about that. I'd like to go in with Mike and a black-and-white unit as backup. And Kemp," he added in what sounded like an afterthought.

"You good with that, Mike?" Loo asked me.

"Absolutely," I answered with no hesitation. I knew it was highly irregular that a person in a consulting capacity would be present for the search and possible arrest of a suspect, but this situation was far from regular. It was also an indication of a certain amount of respect that still existed for me within the detail, despite my ballsy nature.

"Good. I'll coordinate with HBPD. They may want to have a unit there, too," the lieutenant nodded at Hans.

"Fine, but we're not going to need that much backup. If Huntington Beach wants a unit there, then we can leave our patrol unit here. But I'd rather have our own guys if you can swing it, Loo, " Hans said.

"I'll do what I can, but it's their town, Hans."

Hans nodded. Nobody relished the idea of several different departments in a cluster fuck.

"Anything turn up with the rest of the UCLA interviews?" The lieutenant switched subjects.

"Nothing new. The picture we get of Miss Courson remains the same: conservative, reserved, not a lot of friends."

"Any boyfriends crawl out of the woodpile?" he asked.

"No, lieutenant," Hans said. "Nobody new."

"Everybody's heard the results of the Robert Fornier interview by now..." Loo said with a smile.

Chuckles all around. Hans had delighted in telling the story most of the afternoon the day before.

"How about Felicia Vanson?"

Bob Bobb answered. "Dr. Ruffner's tests came back last

night. Both women showed concentrations of booze and LSD."

"That's something, at least."

"Something else may be important to note here as well," Bobb went on. "According to Dr. Ruffner, the strength of the doses must have been very high due to the potency of the sample remaining in their blood. She thinks the Courson girl must have been tripping pretty heavily when she died."

It might also answer how the killer kept his victims under control before he killed them, and further explain the absence of defense wounds or signs of struggle.

"How'd Ruffner come to that conclusion, Bobb?" Townsend asked.

"She used the estimated time of death — the time when the heart would have stopped beating and moving blood through her system — to compare against the potency of the dose that still remained in her bloodstream. Then she worked backwards to the time when Courson probably ingested the dose. Based on the rate the body metabolizes the drug, Dr. Ruffner came to the conclusion that the victim had been tripping on a dose she estimates at about 1500 to 2000 micrograms.s."

"Holy shit," I said. That may well have left permanent brain damage had she survived.

Townsend let out a low whistle of amazement. "She must have been in *space*."

"In light of that," Loo said to Hans, "you may want to talk to your little buddy, Fornier's friend, and find out if he knows anything about whether the trailer guy deals acid, too."

"I'll take care of it first thing," Hans answered.

"There's more," Bobb said. "The New Orleans victim had pretty much the same blood tox. I guess the N.O. cops ran the full shiteree of blood tests on that victim. Anyway, both acid and grass were present there."

"I didn't know that," I said to no one in particular.

Bobb shrugged. "Sorry."

Kemp swallowed the last of his McMuffin. "I've got something."

"Go ahead," Loo directed.

"The DMV rundown on the VW van? Well one of them is registered to that trailer in H.B."

The room went silent. Not only was the suspect at the trailer park alleged to be the one using the apartment whose phone was the recipient of one of Patti Courson's last calls, but the address was now linked to a vehicle at the crime scene.

"*What*?" Hans was incredulous, shaking his head and looking at the floor.

"You didn't say anything about it before now?" It was Loo this time. "It might have expedited the warrant, for Christ sake."

"But I —" Kemp stammered.

At that moment, Rita, the bureau's administrative assistant, came in holding two more pink flimsies, just like last time. She stepped over to the lieutenant and handed them to him.

Loo took the pages, skimmed them briefly, and said, "Looks like we got our warrant, gentlemen. You know what to do. I'll get on the horn with HBPD right away. Check with me in about ten minutes, Hans. In the meantime, go get yourselves ready. Good luck."

*   *   *

HANS DROVE and I rode shotgun. Kemp sat in back.

Conversation was getting more and more sparse as we

neared the Huntington Beach mobile home park. Between the humidity of the cloudy day and the effects of anticipation, I was sweating like a pig.

"Anybody else hot?" I asked.

Hans smiled, noting my tension. We had been through situations like this dozens of times together, and could read each other's thoughts like a book. My former partner said nothing, only reached toward the car's control panel and turned up the air conditioning. I held the lapels of my sport jacket open and leaned into the air vent. The rush of cold air felt good. As I leaned back into the seat, I unconsciously touched the cool handle of my Beretta on the seat between us.

"Is it still there?" Hans asked me. He must have seen my motion, or just as likely, read my mind.

"What? Oh, yeah," I answered his jibe absently. My feeling of foreboding escalated as we closed in on our destination.

Hans sensed my apprehension, and was taking steps to make me more relaxed. The jabs felt familiar and helped me loosen up.

"You awake back there, Dan?" Hans said looking in the rear view mirror.

"Yeah," Kemp said. He had been unusually quiet during the ride.

Hans chuckled. "Whatsamatter? You got low blood sugar or something, Dan?"

"Fuck you," Kemp answered.

Hans laughed again.

I gazed out the window and up at the darkening sky. It was only nine thirty in the morning, but the gloom cast an eerie gray-gold cast on the outdoors. It looked like the effects of a full solar eclipse, and I wondered when it was going to start raining.

A short time later, we pulled into the parking lot of a Union 76 gas station about a mile from the mobile-home park. We were scheduled to rendezvous with the Huntington Beach PD's backup unit there at about ten-fifteen, but they were already there, about ten minutes early. The two officers in the patrol car were inside the service station's convenience store-office, drinking coffee from thick plastic mugs.

Hans introduced himself, then Kemp and me.

I studied the two patrolmen. One, a husky, dark-haired fellow of about thirty-two. The other was small, skinny, with a narrow head and ears that stood straight out.

"I thought you were bringing a uniform unit with you," the husky one said to Hans.

"When we heard you'd be here, we figured we could leave our guys back in L.A. 'to protect and serve'," Hans said. "You up to speed on what's going down this morning?"

"Our sergeant filled us in. Suspect in a serial killing, huh?" Big Ears said.

Hans nodded. "We'd like you guys to lag behind us by about five minutes, okay? I don't want marked cop cars cruising by and spooking this guy before we get there."

"Okay."

We went around to the back of the car, and Hans popped the trunk. Each of the three of us took a Kevlar vest and strapped it on while the uniforms watched.

"When you arrive, wait outside the entrance to the park. We'll call if we need you. And if we need you, come running, code three." Hans was telling them to use their lights and sirens and shag ass fast if we called.

"Got it," they both said.

"All right, let's go," Hans said.

When we got back in the car, Hans said, "Looks like we got Laurel and Hardy backing us up."

"No kidding," I said, a small knot of anxiety tightening in my stomach. Two minutes later we reached the entry of the Seaside Gardens Mobile Home Park, which was neither seaside nor garden-like. We were a good mile and a half from the beach. Four sick-looking palm trees jutted from a berm of green painted rock that surrounded the cinderblock entry wall. The wall was painted yellow, but it had been done long ago, and had faded white, blistered and peeling. Miraculously, taggers had not yet found this target.

We followed the interior streets past dozens of narrow lots, and frail-looking mobile homes. Rust stained many of them, brown tears leaking from joints and nail holes. There was no greenery or plant life around them, only metal mailboxes, cacti and colored pebbles.

Older model compact cars and pickup trucks were parked in confined open carports.

Hans got us to the side of the street and pulled to a stop. The trailer we were looking for was around the corner, the first one on the right. We got out of the car and carefully closed the doors.

The warrant we were serving was a "knock first" warrant, which meant that we couldn't just kick in the back door without first announcing ourselves, allowing the occupant to let us in voluntarily. Most often, this type of warrant gave the occupant the time to flush vital evidence down the toilet. Sometimes you take what you can get.

The knot in my stomach had subsided and a sense of Zen-like connectedness that I remembered from the past, returned to me. Total focus was all that could be read on the faces of all three of us. We drew our guns, and slowly rounded the corner toward the suspect's trailer. I felt a cold wet drop on my forehead and looked to the sky. The clouds had darkened and threatened rain at any moment. Thunder rumbled out over the ocean. Avalon was probably in the middle of a downpour.

The suspect's trailer had once been mint green, but had faded to a light seafoam color. The narrow end faced the street Thin curtains covered two square windows.

The flimsy covered carport was empty and stained with rust, oil and antifreeze. Wooden stairs led to the front door. A wrought-iron handrail was losing the battle with rust along the outer edge of the riser.

Hans signaled to Kemp to cover the back door. Kemp nodded his understanding and crept down the side of the trailer, toward the rear door.

Hans and I gave him a two-minute head start, then approached the entry. This was going to be difficult since the entry stairs were neither big enough, or wide enough, on the landing at the top for two men the size of Hans and me. We couldn't stand on either side of the door.

One of us would have to climb the stairs and stand directly in front of the door, with no room to stand aside should shots be fired from inside. The other would stay at the bottom ready to storm up.

Hans ascended the stairs and cautiously approached the dented aluminum door. I stationed myself behind and to his left, gun held in both hands, the muzzle pointing upward toward the weeping sky.

Hans looked at me, nodded, then rapped sharply on the door. It rattled and banged loosely in its frame as he did so. Hearing nothing from within, he repeated the process. Again there was no response. Nothing at all.

Kemp's head peered from around the corner. Hans nodded to him, and Kemp knocked on the back door. Nothing.

"Police. Open up!" Hans said.

Nothing. Only the sounds of the gathering storm out at sea.

"Open up. We've got a warrant to search these premises, and we're coming in," Hans said authoritatively.

In my peripheral vision, I saw the curtains of the next door unit pull back to reveal a wrinkled and curious face.

There was no response, then *Wham!* It was the sound of heavy weight being slammed against the feeble aluminum walls of the mobile home.

I instinctively ducked into a crouch, Hans did the same. Then the sound came again, then a third time.

The wrinkled face disappeared behind the curtain again.

I looked to my right for the source of the sound, and saw Kemp rearing back over the wooden railing of the back stairs kicking hard against the door, trying to break it in.

"Knock that shit off," Hans said at last. Kemp stopped.

Yamaguchi descended the stairs and shook his head almost imperceptibly as he reached the place where I had crouched, and was now unfurling myself. Together we walked over to the place where Kemp was standing and panting from the effort of his kicks to the door.

Hans stood for a moment at the foot of the stairs, looking first at the door, then at Kemp.

"Notice anything about that door there, Dan?" Hans asked in a condescending tone.

Kemp looked, then turned his head to look blankly at Hans, not understanding. Hans let another couple of seconds elapse.

"The door opens *outward*....see?" he said pointing to the corroded metal flashing that ran around the top, bottom, and side of the door. The fourth side displayed a flimsy set of corroded prefabricated hinges. "You could kick on that fucker all day long and all that'll happen is you'll get tired."

I laughed out loud. Kemp was embarrassed as hell, and said nothing. They say that if you can't laugh at yourself, you leave the job to others.

"Try pulling on the damn thing," Hans said.

Kemp gave it a tug, and nothing happened.

"Hey, Mike, how about trying the front door?"

I did, and it, too, was locked. "You got a crowbar or something in the car?" I asked.

"I think so. Kemp," Hans said as he tossed the car keys to him, "why don't you see if you can find a pry bar or something useful in the trunk, huh?"

*   *   *

KEMP returned in a drizzle of rain. The heavy wet smell of pavement and ozone filled the air.

I wedged the pry bar into the door jamb and jimmied it. It didn't take much to pop it open with a tinny cracking sound.

Guns drawn, we moved into the gloom.

It was modestly furnished with a matching sofa and love seat centered around a coffee table. A cheap television sat on a rolling cart, rabbit-ear antennae perched on the dusty top. A Lay-Z-Boy recliner, an ugly floor lamp, rounded out the room.

It looked like a place occupied by an elderly person of modest means. I looked at Hans with the question in my eyes. *Is this the right place?* Hans shrugged.

Without touching or disturbing anything in anticipation of the coming examination by the criminalist team, we split up and carefully searched the rest of the small home. Kemp took the kitchen, Hans took the living room, and I went down the narrow hallway that ran the length of the mobile home.

The first door I came to was part way open, and I could see that it was a bathroom. I pushed the door with the toe of my shoe, readied my gun, and entered.

It smelled musty and close from mildew and soap. The shower curtains were pulled shut and hung over the edge of the prefabricated tub. *Fuck.* I hate closed shower curtains like this. That Hitchcock thing.

My nerve endings were tingling, and a small bead of sweat ran down the side of my face.

"Open the curtains slowly, and come out," I commanded.

Sounds of Kemp and Hans running to back me up.

"Open up now, goddamn it," I repeated. *Fuck! fuck! fuck! I hate this part.*

I felt them both at my back, guns ready.

In one smooth motion, I leaped to the gap between the shower stall and the toilet, ripping the opaque plastic curtain down from its rings as I made my move. At the same time I brought my gun up, ready to fire.

The shower stall was empty. I released an audible sigh and backed out of the cramped space into the hallway. I nearly ran into Kemp.

"Sorry," I said. "Nobody."

"You scared the shit out of me," he said, and walked back toward the kitchen.

I could hear Kemp opening and closing drawers and cabinets as I moved to the door opposite the bathroom. It was open, and pushed flush against the fake wood-paneled wall in such a way that no one could hide behind it. I moved across the threshold and looked in the closet before looking under the bed.

I used my feet again to slide the hollow wooden closet doors along their runners. Gun drawn and prepared for anything. My breathing got shallower.

Clothes hung limply from their hangers among the faint smell of moth balls, detergent and dust. I pushed the clothes around in the closet and determined that no one was hiding inside, then dropped down to assess the situation under the bed. Nobody home there, either.

I looked about the tiny space, and was suddenly struck by what was missing. Personal effects. There was nothing personal in the house. No photographs, no newspapers, no magazines, no odds and ends that one accumulates and displays. Nothing but outdated furniture and a few hanging pictures that looked like the kind in cheap motels.

The bedroom was no exception. Just clothes, end tables, ceramic lamps beside the queen size bed, a brown bedspread, and a calendar on the wall. It hung from a tiny nail that had been driven into the prefab paneling. It was open to the current month. No markings of any kind had been made on it.

I left the bedroom, reentered the hallway and approached the door to the last room to be checked.

This one was closed. I pushed on it with my foot as before, but met some resistance. Not like someone pushing back, but more like it had been hung too low and rubbed against carpet on the floor. I applied more pressure, raised my gun and pushing hard with my foot.

The door swung open and revealed a dark and stale enclosure that smelled of sulphur and candle wax.

"Holy God," I said out loud. I tried to speak again, my mouth suddenly dry. "Hans, come on back here. I think we've got something."

The sound of Hans feet pounding against the hollow floor of the trailer came immediately. When he reached the doorway, I stood aside to give him a view of what I had found.

The room's only window had been covered over with thick tar paper, the edges taped with black electrician's tape. No light intruded except from the open door behind us. Underneath the darkened window was a simple wooden table, pulled out from an identical, though slightly taller, wooden table. Beneath that was a third, smaller one. The effect resembled stair steps.

It functioned as an altar, framed photos of rock legend Jim Morrison of the Doors were arranged on the top of the altar, and surrounded by a number of thick candles of black, red and white. Many were burned down, melted wax pooled beneath them.

"Jesus, Hans," I said in a whisper. On the bottom rung sat a thick and musty book. Writing of a kind I had never seen adorned thin and chipping pages. It looked like ancient Egyptian or Greek.

Hans didn't respond, instead turned to leave the room.

I made my way back outside into the dark, humid morning, and headed toward the car. I listened to Hans as he spoke into the radio's microphone requesting a team of criminalists and forensic specialists to the scene. The intermittent drizzle of rain felt cool on my clammy skin, and brought me back to reality. The only other sounds besides the crackling response of the police radio was the hum of the street outside the entrance of Seaside Gardens.

I walked toward the entrance to let the Huntington Beach

cops know what had happened, and to thank them for standing by. I needed to do something to clear my head.

I was almost to the park's entrance when the ringing of my cell phone startled me. I reached into the pocket of my coat and withdrew it. I had forgotten to turn it off before we entered the house. That could have been a costly mistake had it made noise when we were trying to surprise a suspect. I chided myself for that oversight and flipped it open to answer the call.

"Mike Travis," I said.

"Mike? It's Trina down at the phone company. How 'ya doing?" she asked in a playful voice.

"I'm fine, Trina. What's going on?"

"You sound funny. Are you okay?" she asked, concerned.

"Yeah, sure I'm fine. I'm just in the middle of something right now is all," I responded, trying to sound normal.

"Well, I've got that address you wanted. Want me to give it to you now, or do you want to call me later?"

"No, go ahead and give it to me now. Wait just a second and let me find something to write on......" I said as I dug into my pocket. "Okay, I'm ready."

"It's thirteen-forty-four Hibiscus Street...." she waited a few moments as I wrote. "...Huntington Beach. Want me to repeat it for you?"

"No," I said hoarsely.

"Mike? Are you okay?" she sounded genuinely worried.

"Yeah. I'm fine. I've gotta go..." I hung up. My heart was in my throat, and I tried to keep it down. My knees felt weak. I was ready to throw up.

I looked back at the trailer. Thirteen-forty-four sat quietly, its door open, Hans standing on the landing talking to Kemp inside.

Chapter Nineteen

THE CAR SLEWED DANGEROUSLY AS I MADE THE hard right turn out of the park. Hans grabbed the dash in front of the shotgun seat for balance. He had barely gotten into the seat before I left Kemp standing with the two HBPD cops in a cloud of exhaust.

"*Fuck!*" I pounded the wheel.

The rain was beginning to come harder as I approached the freeway on ramp.

"What the hell's happening, Travis?"

"I know where he is. We've got to get to Avalon. *Now.*"

Hans had his hand on the radio mike before I finished. He needed no further explanation. We were partners.

"Patch me through to Lieutenant Delano right away."

Electric tension filled the car, jagged energy, like the storm. Seconds stretched, stretched.

"Delano. Go ahead," Loo's voice said.

"Yamaguchi here, Lieutenant. We have reason to believe the suspect we are looking for is presently offshore. Request helicopter transport and backup in LASO jurisdiction."

For a moment, nothing. Static.

I knew Loo was trying to decipher Hans' cryptic message. The media had police scanners. We didn't need any complications.

"Your suspect. He's on a boat?" Loo asked after what seemed like minutes.

"Negative," Hans said. "Small town. Repeat, small town."

Brake lights glowed on the freeway ahead, and I squeezed the wheel in frustration.

"Roger that. I'll get back to you in two."

"Ten-four." Hans kept hold of the mike and looked at me. The muscles of his jaw worked as he clenched his teeth.

"I'm taking us to Long Beach Harbor, Hans. If Loo can't get us a chopper, we're going to need a backup plan."

His eyes were unblinking. "What's going on, Travis?"

"The call I just got was from a friend at the phone company. I was getting an address for a friend of mine in Avalon. She was looking for her brother."

"Her brother?"

The tires hummed and I could feel us begin to hydroplane on the wet freeway. I accelerated anyway, threading my way through a knot of traffic just ahead. A horn blared loudly as I cut too quickly into the right line.

"She'd never met him before. She's adopted."

"And the trailer was the address you came up with?" Hans was incredulous.

I didn't take my eyes from the road and accelerated onto the right shoulder to pass again.

"She was going to get in contact with the guy. I already

found the phone number for her. Gave it to her yesterday." I was assaulted by guilt at the memory. What if I hadn't taken her to dinner? If I hadn't pried into her life? If I hadn't encouraged her to find her family. If, if, if....

The radio squealed, called out unit number.

Hans punched the button. "Yamaguchi."

"Delano here. Negative on air transport. Repeat, negative on air transport."

Shit!

Lightning strobed the dark sky off to the west, over Catalina. Hans looked at me.

"Then we'll go private," I said.

I punched the accelerator and sped toward the Long Beach exit. More horns. Fuck 'em.

"Roger, Lieutenant. We're proceeding code two to Long Beach Harbor," Hans said into the mike. Code two. Proceeding urgently. "Will call on arrival."

"Ten-four. LASO backup is standing by."

I tossed Hans my cell phone. "Dial a number for me." I had to warn Deana against making contact with her brother. *What have I done?*

It was ringing when he handed it back. I saw another flash of lightning over the ocean. A sharp crack of static interrupted the signal on my phone.

"Pete's Roadhouse," came the answer.

"Pete?" I asked.

"Yeah. Who's this?"

"Pete, this is Mike Travis, look —"

"Hey 'ya Mikey.

I tried to sound in control. "Look, I'm in kind of a hurry, is Deana there?"

"No, and I'll tell 'ya what, I wish she was. It's raining like hell, and all the tourists are either holed up in their hotels or drinking in the bars. I'm busy as a one-legged man in an ass-kicking contest —"

"Where is she?" I interrupted.

"Damned if I know. She's probably showing her brother around. Said he was coming over to meet her. She seemed pretty excited, you know? I guess she didn't even know she *had* a brother until —"

"When...when was this? When did he come over?" I think I was shouting.

"Whoa, Mikey, relax," Pete said.

"Look, I don't have time to explain. Deana's in trouble. The guy she's with is *bad*. Dangerous. I need to know where she is — how to get in touch with her.."

"I really don't know. Try her at home. If you want me to, I'll send one of the guys to go get her. Hell, Yosemite's right here—"

"*No*! That's going to be too dangerous. I'll handle it on this end. Just call me *immediately* if you find out where she is. I mean it. Call me right away, okay?" He had my number.

I took the Long Beach Harbor exit. The tires barely held the road.

"She's next, Hans. God *damn* it!"

"How can you be so sure?" He was trying to calm me down. Partners.

"It's about blood offerings. It's what Jacquie Whitney and I were talking about. And now he's got a chance to sacrifice his own flesh and blood."

Hans stared at me.

"Toss me the phone," I said.

I punched in Information. Thirty seconds later I got the

number I was looking for and dialed it.

"Island Helicopters. How can I help you, please?" The voice was that of a pleasant-sounding young woman.

"Where are you located, please?" The woman gave me the address. I was reasonably certain I knew how to get there, but got directions anyway. No time for fuck-ups.

"When is your next departure?" I asked.

"It depends on the weather, sir. We don't fly in heavy wind or rain."

"Are you flying *now*?" I asked.

"Yes, but as I said, if the weather warrants it, we will ground our flights —"

"I would like to know when your next departure *is*." I had exhausted any pretense of self-control.

"Every thirty minutes, *sir*," she began in an exasperated tone, "at fifteen and forty-five after the hour."

I hung up and looked at my watch. Five minutes would put me at their door. Nothing was going to keep me from getting back to Avalon. Nothing.

The son of a bitch was on my island.

*   *   *

AS THE CAR rolled to a stop, I leaped clear and ran across the expanse of black tarmac, slick with the combination of oil and rain. Two six-passenger Bell helicopters sat idle.

The air was a heavy drizzle. It smelled of the sea and roiled on gusts of wind. I banged my way in to the office, Hans right behind me.

A Formica counter and an overweight woman. She sat on a desk chair much too short for the counter. Her eyes were wide at my entrance.

"I spoke to you on the phone a few minutes ago. I am work-ing with the Los Angeles Police Department. My partner and I need immediate transportation to Avalon."

The fat woman was shaking her head before I finished.

"I'm sorry, sir, but as I told you on the phone, we are sub-ject to cancellations in inclement weather. We are grounded. No flights until further notice."

My neck felt hot as anger rose. I hadn't been there for Reggie Carter, and now he was dead. I was not going to lose Deana, too.

Two skinny long-haired men in their mid-forties leaned against the wall toward the rear corner of the building and sipped coffee out of Styrofoam cups. They were watching the exchange.

"This is a *police emergency*. We need —"

"I *am* sorry, sir. That's policy."

"I don't think you understand —" I felt myself begin to slip away.

"Listen, asshole. I don't care *who* you are. We're fucking *grounded*. We don't *fly*. We're *not* —"

The barrel of my Beretta caught the bridge of his nose. Blood flowed freely as I shoved him against the wall. I pressed the gunsight up under his eye socket. He hung there.

"You're gonna fly!"

"Aaaagh!"

It was Hans who pulled me down. He pressed his fingers into the nerve on my wrist. "Easy, Mike. Easy."

The front of the chopper pilot's shirt was soaked red.

"He tried to fucking kill me!" One eye squinted, already bluing in hemorrhaging blood.

"If I was trying to kill you, you'd be dead," I said.

"We need a way to Avalon," Hans said.

The other pilot spoke quickly. "The ferry. Over there across the parking lot.."

"I'm gonna sue your ass —"

Hans gave the injured man his business card. "Take it up with me later. You've got witnesses. You should do real well."

I watched Hans smile. It was not pretty.

We ran toward the dock about a hundred yards away. Passengers were already ascending the ramp that stretched from the wide wooden wharf and into the eighty-foot power craft tied along side.

Hans badged the girl taking tickets, and we passed inside. He stepped into a shallow alcove and put my cell phone to his ear. I stared out into the slanting rain and waited.

"Did you reach Loo?" I asked when he rang off.

"Yeah. He's contacted the Sheriff's office and got us some help on arrival in Avalon. We'll be working with the locals only. Weather's gonna prevent sending a SWAT team over. By the way, Loo says they grounded our choppers, too, if it makes you feel any better."

"It doesn't, but that's what I figured, " I said.

"Me either."

*   *   *

THE *ISLAND LADY* shuttled as many as one hundred and fifty passengers at a time between the Port of Long Beach and Avalon Harbor on Catalina Island, across the channel. The boat was sold out, as was common during the busy summer season.

The passage normally took about forty-five minutes, but the weather would adversely affect that. And with so much riding on our getting to Deana in time the trip would feel like a lifetime. I just hoped it didn't take what remained of Deana's.

I found two seats at a table near the stern of the boat. Hans made his way forward through the crowd for some coffee. I used the time to review, to think. Things I had learned from *Rolling Stone* magazine.

"The Lizard King" reference had its origins in an epic poem by Morrison called *Celebration of the Lizard* which had appeared in print inside one of the Doors' album jackets. The killer's reptilian images were obviously related to that.

The article talked about Morrison's persona. Somehow he engendered near-worship among huge numbers of people. To this day, thousands every month still visited his grave outside Paris. People close to him even referred to him as Dionysius, the Greek god of wine and pleasure.

Hans returned with two steaming cups and sat down facing me.

"What's going on, Travis?"

"It's all about Jim Morrison, the singer for the Doors."

Hans' face melted into a sour look of disbelief. "But he's dead."

"I don't know if I understand it all, either. Yet. But our guy seems to be killing people in all the places that had significance in Morrison's life. Like human sacrifices."

Hans stared at me.

"Today is July third, the day he died. July 3, 1971. Based on what I read, there was only one person who allegedly saw Morrison's body placed into its casket and buried. His wife, Pamela Courson. Before any of Jim's friends or family could reach Paris, they were told he had already been buried. Pamela died just a few years later."

"Courson," Hans said. "That's a hell of a coincidence."

I was making a fist and staring at it.

"Try to get through the next few minutes, Travis."

"Rumor had it," I said, "that he staged his own death so he could be free of rock stardom. He wanted to be a poet. Pursue his muse."

"What does that have to do with this?"

"There were people who said he was a demigod, immortal even, someone whose spirit might now inhabit a different soul. The incarnation of Dionysius. Remember your mythology?"

"Dionysius was the Greek god of wine and fertility. Also called the Twin or the Twice Born. He was born once from his mortal mother, then again from the thigh of his father, the god Zeus. Religious cults worshipping Dionysius were so grossly immoral and depraved that even the ancient Romans tried to ban them."

I stared at him. "How did you know all that?"

"What, you think you're the only one with an education?"

I made a fist again, crushing my fingers together, nails biting the flesh of my palm.

"There's more, you know," I said. "When Dionysius grew to adulthood, he went down to Hades itself to rescue his dead mother. He brought her back to life and placed her on a throne beside his father."

"The sacrificial shit. The stuff you and Jacquie talked about."

"I think so. I think this is all about resurrection. Eternal life."

"What does that have to do with our freak?"

"The killer's mother is dying."

The throb of the boat's engines pulsed up through the deck. The boat vibrated. I noticed some passengers were beginning to look ill from diesel exhaust and the rolling sea.

I looked at Hans. "You feeling okay?"

"Yeah, fine. I think I need to walk around or something." He got up, leaving his coffee on the table.

I had learned, too, that Morrison had claimed to have been inhabited by the spirit of an American Indian shaman who had entered his pre-teen body as he and his family passed the scene of a bloody automobile accident that had caused the deaths of a number of Indian passengers. That incident had taken place on a lonely stretch of highway somewhere between Santa Fe and Albuquerque, New Mexico. The location where our killer's first victim had been found.

Morrison's estranged relationship with his own Navy Admiral father could well have been the link established with the first victim's having been a military man. The only victim to have been mutilated.

Images assailed me: The note found on the hotel matchbook in Phoenix, *My dusky jewel*, it had read. Lyrics from a Doors song penned by Morrison. Another note had read, *The Scream of the Butterfly*. Another lyric.

A UCLA coed dead, her body found on the campus itself. The place where Morrison had attended film school. The victim's name was Pamela, just as Morrison's wife's had been.

More impressions flooded in: a lizard's clawed foot clutching a dagger; the wings of a butterfly morphing into the wings of an angel; the agonized face of a woman from whose womb crawled a reptile grasping a dagger....

Hans had reappeared beside me looking queasy. "Shouldn't be much longer."

I stared out the rain-streaked window at the black sky. "It better not be."

*   *   *

IT TOOK the *Island Lady* over an hour-and-a-half to cross.

As the crew finished securing the mooring lines, passengers scuttled to the ramps to disembark. Hans and I bullied our way to the front of the line with muttered apologies.

We were met at the foot of the gangplank by my Harbor Patrol buddy, Art Lund, and two L.A Sheriff's deputies, all in uniform. They stood beneath streaming black umbrellas, the drumbeats of large raindrops heavily smacking their slick surfaces.

"Is there a place we can talk?" Hans asked no one in particular.

"Let's head to the office," one of the deputies said. "It's only a couple of blocks."

We climbed into a GMC Suburban painted in the two tones of a Sheriff's patrol unit, a light-bar on the roof. We made our way past the crowd at the wharf while the deputies introduced themselves.

The driver was a stocky, balding man with a thick brown mustache, who kept watching me in the rear view mirror. His name was Rick Johnson. The other deputy was Jim Cox.

Loo had briefed them over the phone as Hans and I had made our way across the channel. So I began with the essence of my theory about the killer's motivation, and how I knew Deana was the next likely target. I explained how the brother and sister had planned to meet that day.

Hans and I spelled out to the others where we thought we should begin our search. Bad weather meant an overnight stay, so no more channel crossings were going to be made until the storm cleared. The obvious first choice was Deana's apartment. If we didn't find them there, I knew the odds of finding the hotel where the killer would have holed up were virtually nil, since he would use an assumed name and pay cash.

There hadn't been time to access a photo of the suspect, and I now wished we had something we could use while checking the town's hotels and motels. Time was bleeding away. Another false god.

The team constructed a list of the possible locations that the psychopath might conduct his ritual. We believed that it would need to be a place that could offer enough seclusion that the sacrifice could be carried out over the course of several hours, but minimizing the risk of interruption or detection. The prior killings had taken that kind of time.

The limited size of the seaside town and the absence of any network of real roads were about the only things working in our favor. The killer was limited to an area within Avalon's boundaries. The weather would also keep him close by.

"The weather's gonna rule out anyplace outdoors, don't you think?" Cox put in.

"I think that's right," Hans said.

"I agree." I said. "The past victims all appeared to have been killed indoors, then dumped. It makes sense, especially given the time that he probably takes with his victims. LSD appears to be a factor in these killings as well. He doses them pretty heavily, so I don't think you'd want an intended victim freaking out and getting away from you outdoors."

"Somewhere controllable, but off the beaten path..." Johnson said, thinking aloud.

"And I think there's an importance attached to the site that has to correspond with Morrison, the Doors, or their music somehow. Did they ever play here?"

"Not that I heard," Cox answered. "But I'm not sure."

"I heard he was here once," Johnson said. "Morrison, I'm talking about. I thought the band had a boat or something."

"Could be. But if so, there could be a thousand places the guy might have come and hung out," I said. "*Shit.*"

The GMC went silent as we wracked our brains. It was time to act. Time to try *something*. Anything.

"Fuck it. Let's get to her apartment. We've got to try that first," I said impatiently.

"We'll stop at the office first," Cox said. "Art, you stick by the phone in case something comes through from the mainland. We'll keep you posted by radio."

Art nodded.

"Let's do it," Hans agreed.

Johnson parked the car outside a nondescript building, and we walked briskly through the gathering rain. The room was close and hot.

I briefed them on what I remembered of Deana's apartment building using the dry-erase marker board hanging on the wall, and worked up an action plan for the four of us. When we were finished, we got back into the Suburban and made our way through the town's wet winding streets toward the Spanish-style building where I hoped to find Deana, alive and alone.

The dark sky had activated the streetlights. Raindrops pelted through orange light. I knew I would never forget this rain, never like the rain again.

The streets were deserted, everyone indoors, inside hotels, restaurants and bars. The only indication of the presence of humanity. The seaside village was a ghost town.

*   *   *

RICK Johnson parked the Suburban in a red zone near the entrance of Deana's apartment building. Rain had turned the white stucco to a soggy gray. Yellow light shone from apartment windows.

The old-style layout of the building was going to make our entrance difficult. There was no back door, which left the poorly lit narrow hallway as our only way in.

Single file, we approached Deana's door. I could see a faint pattern of light from the window. *Please be here*, I thought to myself.

I raised my hand in a "stop" signal at the lighted window. I listened for any sound from inside, but heard none. I reached for the door handle and twisted. It met immediate resistance against the lock.

I looked at the window again. She had left it open. Old habits died hard. My hand closed on the cool steel of the knob.

I motioned Hans with my head toward the other side of the door. He moved quickly into position. First one in. He drew his pistol, held it in both hands, and watched me.

I twisted the knob.

A faint *click* of the latch, followed instantly by Hans' shoving the door open. Crossing the threshold he swung his pistol, back and forth, covering any potential field of threatening fire. Cox, Johnson and I went in after him.

Yamaguchi's heavy footfalls could be felt through the floor as he rushed to find Deana. Or the killer. Johnson and I remained in the front as Cox followed my old partner toward the back.

Two wine glasses, used and empty, sitting in the sink. I looked under the sink, pulled out the plastic trash can, and peered in. Two empty bottles of cheap chablis.

"They've been here," I called out.

Hans and Cox returned to the entry area. Hans was shaking his head, and holding something in his hand. "This isn't good."

I looked him. He had found Deana's purse. "Shit."

"It was sitting on her bed," Hans said.

A stony silence fell over the room.

"We ought to call Art and see if he's heard anything," Johnson said. "There's no sense in running around half-cocked."

I reached into my jacket pocket, withdrew my phone, and handed it to the stocky deputy. He punched in the numbers, spoke briefly to Art, then looked at me.

"Just flip it closed," I said. He did and handed it back.

"Nothing so far," he said.

I had to *do* something! *Think!*

I thought about the bell tower on the hillside. No. Outdoors. The old Wrigley Mansion? Too many people. It had been turned into a bed-and-breakfast.

What would I do? Where would I go? Somewhere symbolic...

And it came. Like an epiphany. I went cold, and deadly calm.

"I know where he is," I said.

*   *   *

PROBABLY the most prominent and recognizable of Avalon's landmarks is the famous Casino building. Opened in the late

1920's, the circular art deco building became a popular venue for big-band concerts, dances and balls. Shaped like a roulette wheel twelve stories tall, it now houses a museum, movie theater and an art gallery. The long abandoned main ballroom, replete with gilded stage and parquet floor, is rarely ever used and only available to the public for infrequent special events.

The decorative archways were bathed in light from within, and stood out against the black backdrop of clouds and rain.

The Suburban's wipers swept sheets of water from the windshield. They barely kept up with the torrential squall. We skidded to a stop on the concrete walkway. There was not a soul in sight.

The sound of our running feet echoed loudly on the promenade. We raced around in a wide half circle until we reached the glass doors, the entrance to the foyer of the Grand Ballroom.

I pulled on one of the handles and the door came open. It had been jimmied in such a way that it was unlikely to be discovered by any but the most observant of security guards or passers by.

"He's here," I said. "The sonofabitch is here."

The four of us entered the anteroom, sucking down our labored breathing. Weapons ready, we fanned out. Hans and I to the oversized ballroom doors to the right of where we stood, Johnson and Cox to the left.

Faded red carpet muffled our steps. There was no light to guide our way other than what filtered in from the stormy outdoors. There was a haunting and lonely sense to the place. Ghosts of revelers dressed in tuxedos and long gowns whispered in dusty and neglected recesses, seeking to restore the spirit of what had been lost to time.

Faint strains of music echoed from within the empty ballroom. I slowly opened the heavy door that separated us from the grand room, and as I did, the music became clearer.

I recognized the tune. It was a discordant and acid-drenched passage from the Doors' *Not to Touch the Earth.*

The room was enormous, more so because of its emptiness. A sea of polished hardwood was surrounded by a half-circle of red and gold carpeting. Dozens of circular tables, chairs upside down, scarred and covered in dust. Immense chandeliers hung from the ceiling that rose at least three stories above us. Two of these were dimly illuminated, throwing an odd brownish light about the center of the dance floor, leaving the periphery in deep shadow.

Morrison's voice amplified in the vast empty space. I squinted in the dimness to find the source of faint scrambling off to my left. I saw Johnson and Cox.

We were all focused on the shapes that occupied center stage, against a two-story backdrop of plush, deep red. Candlelight glowed waveringly over the heavy curtains, and made a dramatic shadow dance on the crushed velvet.

We moved closer. Eyes finally adjusting to the dimness.

I made out the shape of a man, kneeling and hunched, swaying rhythmically from side to side as if being rocked on a gentle sea, his back to the dance floor across which we approached. A recumbent form lay in front of him, unmoving, bare legs illuminated against the darkness, the torso hidden behind him where he knelt.

It was a smooth target acquisition, the man's head in the sights of my Beretta.

Make a move you sick bastard. Light my fire.

In my peripheral vision I saw Hans, weapon drawn and ready, just ten feet to the right and slightly behind me. The two

Sheriff's deputies were farther back, still off to my left.

Capture alive, the manual says. Preserve life. Lethal force only as a last resort.

We closed in.

The stage was raised about three feet above the level of the floor, and I had to raise the angle of the Beretta with every step of my approach. I was only five yards from the platform when I noticed the head of the reclining form turn slowly toward me, and Deana opened her eyes.

Keep quiet. Say nothing.

The lids of her vacant eyes slowly fell shut again. Not a glimmer of recognition or focus.

I now closed to about ten feet when, all at once, Deana's eyes flew open, as if only then recognizing me. She let out a terrifying scream.

The killer's head snapped around reflexively.

"Don't move! Down on the ground, motherfucker! *Do* it! *Now!*" I yelled.

His eyes were wild, crazed, stoned out of his mind. Deana was shrieking with terror, the noise blending in counterpoint with Morrison's words. She raised both hands to her face as she screamed, leaving a viscous bloody smudge on her mouth and chin. Her left hand was deeply cut and bleeding badly.

The killer unwound from his kneeling position and turned to face me. In his right hand was a long slender blade. He smiled a deranged smile. Even in the semi-dark of the huge ballroom, I could see his teeth and lips were stained red.

"In any generation, there can be only one..." he rasped.

"Down! *Now!*" My gun was trained on his heaving chest. He was excited.

"Drop the knife, and get down on the goddamn floor!" Hans

said as he took long strides, closing on the killer.

The deputies' weapons were aimed at the man as well, feet spaced apart in the classic stance.

The killer made no move to drop his weapon, but went into a crouch. Time slowed to a crawl again, and adrenaline pumped ice through my veins. He looked as though he was giving up.

His knees bent further, then suddenly, he leaped toward me from the edge of the stage, knife slicing the air as he flew.

I two-tapped the Beretta, knocking him around like a rag doll.

Muzzle flash, smoke, the Doors spinning out their reality, Deana screaming.

The flashes in the darkened room briefly blinded me, and the sounds of gunfire mixed with a continuous din of terrified screams. Deana was writhing on the stage.

He flew across the empty space between us. My back and head hit the floor hard, sending a burst of bright light exploding through my brain, momentarily dazing me. I scrambled out from under the weight of the man on top of me, and his head made a ripe-melon sound as it hit the floor.

My chest was heaving, but I raised the gun to aim at the man who lay at my feet, face up, a dime-sized entrance wound in the center of his forehead.

Mine.

His eyes were wide and staring, tongue, lips and teeth red with the blood he had been sucking from the wound he had sliced in Deana's left hand before we arrived. He looked different without his black leather jacket.

Deana kept writhing and shrieking even as Hans propped her up, holding her gently and stroking her wet and matted hair. "You're all right, now. It's okay. It's okay," Hans crooned softly.

I tore a sleeve off my shirt and bound up her hand.

A haze of smoke and pungent cordite hung in the still air of the old ballroom, dimly illuminated by chandeliers and candle-light.

Epilogue

OCTOBER IN AVALON WAS GRAY AND COLD. THE crush of tourists had returned to their homes. The beach beside the pier empty save for the squawking of seagulls fighting over scraps and garbage.

I pulled my Navy peacoat tight around me, steeling myself against the wind that blew across the bow of the *Kehau,* and tried unsuccessfully to clear my mind.

The solution of the "Lizard King Murders," as the press took to calling them, was a spectacular circus for weeks after the bloody climax at the Avalon Casino. Not a day went by when my picture, or Hans Yamaguchi's, wasn't appearing on the TV news accompanied by grim footage of the killer's body being removed from the old grand ballroom.

Internet sites appeared virtually overnight, and offered all sorts of facts and speculation as to the motivation of the newly infamous serial killer, James Douglas Porter.

Hans was a hero. And so was I, I guess. But I sure as hell didn't feel like one.

I had attended the funeral of my mentor and friend, Reginald Carter. After it was over, I sat at his graveside and told him about my life in the years that had encroached since we had ridden together in a squad car. I had always meant to visit him after his retirement, maybe buy him a few beers or go sailing on the *Kehau*. So many meant-to's in my life. Two hours later, I toasted the old man, took one last swig, and poured the bottom half of a fifth of Cutty Sark onto the grass beside his headstone. His favorite.

The old green and white VW van had been registered to James Porter and was found in a public parking lot near the wharf from which the *Island Lady* made its daily departures for Catalina Island. The forensics team found trace evidence of blood from at least four of the victims in it. He had killed them in the back of his van and later dumped the bodies, as we had suspected.

Porter's trailer had been searched and over sixteen ounces of marijuana were found, together with numerous blotters of LSD and three full ounces of crystal meth.

It was never proven whether his mother, Kelsey Anne Porter, had known anything about her son's activities. I believed she had. As she lay dying of cancer, her son's sacrificial murders fit too well with the ancient Dionysian myth to be ignored. I believed she wanted her son to resurrect her. She never came out of her coma, and died the very same day I had shot her son.

The hippie from Hinano's was picked up off the BOLO we issued and held in police custody for nearly twelve hours while Hans and I had been in Avalon. His name was Jason Landry and was a simple working man guilty of nothing more than being a barfly and occasionally scoring a little weed from Porter. I guessed he would parlay his story of being peripherally involved in the case into free drinks for the next couple of weeks.

Representatives of Jim Morrison's estate, as well as the other Doors, were careful and wise in their denouncement of any responsibility for the gruesome murders. Any public figures having a mass audience as widespread as they, with art and music as powerful as theirs, could just as easily become the object of misplaced adoration and worship.

The Doors were only guilty of deeply affecting their audience, nothing more. And that is precisely the goal of worthwhile art: to disturb us from our doldrums. I had said so publicly at every opportunity.

All I wanted to do now was get on with my retirement; maybe take my own sweet time and sail the *Kehau* around the world. It had always been a dream of mine, and it seemed the right time to chase the dreams of the living rather than the ghosts of the dead.

*   *   *

I LOOKED up at the family's house high on the hill, squinting from the sun as it slipped behind the low hills that surrounded Avalon. Deana had already been gone for about a week.

It had been necessary to admit her to a psych ward at a private hospital on the mainland to treat her for LSD-induced psychosis, due to the massive dose James Douglas Porter had forced on her.

When Deana was released, I had been there to bring her back

home to Catalina.

She was subdued and withdrawn, the light in her eyes dimmed, though she sometimes smiled and offered small tokens of gratitude in the forms of softly brushing her fingertips against my suntanned cheeks or gently squeezing my hand. She was like a shy young child, and spoke very little. The essence of her had been burned away by the LSD and the trauma, and it broke my heart whenever I looked at her.

I felt strangely responsible for what had happened to Deana, though I knew that others may well have been killed had I never uncovered the connection between her and Porter. It was the only solace that allowed me to sleep at night. My own nightmares had almost become friends.

I had taken her into my family's home on the hill, and together with the caretakers, had done everything I could to coax back her once sweet and lively spirit. Deana's physical wounds, deep slashes to her left palm, had healed in a matter of weeks, though her delicate hand remained stiff and clawlike. It would probably never open all the way because of the severe nerve damage inflicted on it.

One afternoon, Pete, Rex, Singin'Dude, Mike, and Yosemite Sam came up to the house and brought Deana a beautiful bouquet of flowers and a card that had been signed by all the regulars down at Pete's Roadhouse. The card said how much they missed and cared about her. She took the flowers and placed them in a vase on the table in the kitchen.

Rex and Yosemite were so overcome that they had to wait outside. They couldn't stand to see what Deana had become. The others lingered for a while, though she never appeared to remember them.

Several nights later, though, I sneaked quietly into her room to check in on her long after she had gone to bed. The card they had given her was clutched in her hand as she slept. Even now, with her gone, I keep it. It rests in the drawer of the night-stand next to my bed.

Deana and I spent over a month together in that house. The doctors had said she needed a soft landing back to reality, and to the things that had once been familiar and safe. I wanted that for her too, but after a month had come and gone, she told me she wanted to go "home."

Days later I found myself holding her face in my hands, kissing her softly on the lips, just before she ducked under the swirling rotors that sent the long wisps of dark brown hair flying about her, and climbed into the noisy helicopter and flew away to the mainland and her return to Pomona.

She was going to live with her mother for a while. Her adoptive mother. Mary Woods. Her *family.*

I never let her see my tears.

Author's Note

The Doors' appearance at the Whisky A Go Go and the release of the *LA Woman* album are dealt with anachronistically. That album was released at least a year later than is portrayed in this story, and I am not aware that there was ever any such release party, let alone an heir to Jim Morrison.

This story is purely fictional, however the power and importance of the Doors' music is very real. They left an indelible mark on rock history, and in addition to a peerless body of musical work, there are a number of great books by and about the band that are both entertaining and fascinating. Thank you John Densmore, Robbie Krieger, Ray Manzarek, and Jim Morrison.

If you enjoyed Roadhouse Blues, you won't
want to miss Baron R. Birtcher's newest
noir thriller featuring Mike Travis.

RUBY TUESDAY

Turn the page for an excerpt from this
captivating new novel. Coming from
Durban House in the spring of 2001.

AN EXCERPT FROM THE FORTHCOMING NOVEL

RUBY TUESDAY

BY BARON R. BIRTCHER

I GROPED BLINDLY FOR THE TAG HEUER DIVER'S watch I keep on the nightstand. Not there.

My headache pounded. I pried my reluctant eyes open and finally located it attached to my wrist. 4:33a.m. Heavy rain beat against the teak deck above, and the *Kehau* moved restlessly against her mooring.

I sat upright amidst a clammy tangle of sheets, ran my fingers through damp hair. My pulse drummed behind my eyeballs, my mouth tasted raw.

Red eyes gazed back at me as I splashed cool water on my face. A little too much celebration at Lola's. It was all coming back.

I brushed my teeth, and opened the portholes in my stateroom. The Hawaiian air felt cool against my sun-browned skin.

I crept down the companionway to check on my crew. Loud snores came from both guest staterooms. Good. Rex and Dave were both aboard. I sure as hell didn't remember coming back from the bar.

I climbed the stairs to the galley, passed amid a static hiss from the VHF radio that I always monitor, and went on deck to see if my skiff, the *Chingadera*, was tied alongside. It was, but I didn't remember doing *that* either. I watched it bob and tug with the rhythm of my pounding head. It was going to be a long day.

I sat cross-legged on the deck and let the rain drench me.
The heavy drops soaked me to the skin, but it felt good to
have something natural, something normal and grounding,
happening to me. I needed to reorient myself after the previous night's debauch. The first night in port after a ten-day
crossing from California to Hawaii. Avalon to Kona.
Another twenty five hundred miles between my old life and
the new one. Between LAPD Homicide and me.

After a half hour or so, I went below, toweled off, then
dressed in a pair of shorts and olive green T-shirt. By the time
I returned to the galley, I felt my shirt beginning to stick to
my back despite the air conditioning inside. I found a bottle
of aspirin, shook out three tablets, and washed them down
with a cold Asahi.

The beer stung my raw stomach.

I opened a can of tomato juice, poured it into a large tumbler, threw in handful of ice and filled the rest with Asahi.
My old standby hangover remedy. Hair of the dog.

By five-thirty the rain had stopped. Patches of purple sky
glowed between the parting clouds. Dawn. My talisman. I
took a towel to the afterdeck, wiped down a space, and lay
down in the cool morning air.

I must have fallen asleep, because the sun was well over
Hualalai volcano when I reopened my eyes. I stood up with a
commendable sense of balance, then went below to fire up
my laptop. After logging on through the on-board satellite
system, I checked for any e-mail, then got my day under
way.

I had planned on making the hour-long drive to check on
my family's old beach house, and seeing my childhood

friend, Tino Orlandella.   Hadn't seen the place in over twenty years. It was a pilgrimage.

*　　*　　*

I TURNED off the main highway onto a one lane surface road that veered off toward the ragged coastline. I worked through the sharp twists and turns. Dense groves of coffee and macadamia nuts blanketed the mountain behind me. Spindly trunks of papaya and palms spread out ahead amid purple and white orchids growing wild along the road.

About four miles down toward the ocean, a yellow sign marked the entrance to a private road where the pavement turned to dirt. A canopy of ohia overgrew the road and formed a tunnel. Pinpoints of midmorning sun filtered through and dotted the road.   Imprints of tires were visible in red-brown earth. About two hundred yards on, the road ended in a cul-de-sac carved from a coconut grove.

I parked and rolled down the window, letting the engine idle. The fragrance of plumeria filled the air and triggered a rush of memories. Memories I had called upon for years, retreated to, when times were bad.

But it was harder than I thought, coming back. I could still see the red strobes of the ambulance on the side of the house. The cops. My mother's shrouded body. But the place held power. An indelible piece of my past, laid down like tire treads.

I looked off into the shady space between our house and that of our neighbor, Tino, and recalled happier times. Games of war we played as kids. Later it was spin-the-bottle with Ruby Duke and Laura de Stefano. The excitement of first touch, the innocence of it.

I could remember the first time I felt I was *in love*. With Ruby. The summer I turned sixteen. My mother was dead, and my father, brother and I had returned for the first time since. It wasn't the same. It was never the same again, and we rarely returned after that.

Tino and Ruby had long since married and lived in the house given them by Tino's family. It had been a long time since I had seen them.

Tino was a construction worker by trade, but looked after my family's house in a casual arrangement where he would let either my brother or me know if anything needed repair. Tino wanted nothing in exchange. A friend. But I always saw to it that they were taken care of every Christmas.

Our house was simple, two stories, constructed in the late 1950's; basically a large square with a wide lanai surrounding the front and sides. Oversized windows opened onto a tranquil lagoon. Red and yellow hibiscus surrounded the wooden railing that ran the perimeter of the lanai.

I switched off the ignition. A brief silence was overtaken by the clatter of mynah birds. I stepped from the car and walked barefooted across the sandy soil to the door of my family's plantation-style house.

I took out a key and inserted it into the keyhole. As I turned it, the door abruptly swung inward. A stink of old cigarettes and stale liquor assaulted me and a shirtless man wearing faded cutoffs peered through the screen. His hair was tousled and unkempt, eyes yellow and bloodshot.

"Haul ass," he said, shutting the door. The voice was like gravel. "Get the hell outta here."

Cold rage surged. This place was almost sacred to me.

I pulled the screen open and pushed through. He jumped back just in time to keep from being hit by the swinging door.

"Who the fuck you think you are, dude?" he said. Surly, but shaken.

"You're in my house, asshole." I planted my feet, ready to put out the guy's lights. I was expecting him to throw a punch, but he surprised me by laughing instead.

"Fuck off," he said, and began to shut the door again.

I took hold of his unshaven neck. I found the nerve ends, dug in, and walked him backward. I bounced him off the couch and he landed hard on the floor.

My stomach heaved. The room was musty and closed, littered with empty bottles. The only fresh air came in through the door behind me.

"How about we start over?" I said.

The man rubbed his throat and eyed me furiously. He pushed his words around the bruises. "Do— Do you know who I *am*?"

"No. I thought you understood that."

"I'm Danny Webb."

I shrugged.

"Fuck you, man. I'm a guest of Belden Van de Groot. It's his house." I should have guessed. My brother and I don't always communicate well.

"You're the rock star," I said. He looked familiar, but hard living had left its mark. Keith Richards without the class.

"Yeah. That's right." Self-importance lit in his bloodshot eyes. It was a look his face was comfortable with.

"I thought you were *dead*." I didn't really. But he looked like he was working at it. And using my family's house to do it.

He rubbed his throat angrily. "You fucked up my vocal chords."

"Nothing permanent."

He started to stand up.

I took a long step and pushed hard on the top of his head. He slammed back to the floor. His face turned an angry red.

"I'm Belden's brother, the *other* owner of this house. Now just sit tight there, friend, and we'll get this taken care of."

He took out a pack of cigarettes and lighter, shook one loose, and pulled it from the package with his dry lips.

"No," I said.

Webb glared, then put the cigarette in a dirty ashtray, unlit.

I kicked through a pile of dirty laundry and walked to the phone in the kitchen. I punched out the number for VGC's New York headquarters.

"Van de Groot Capital," a nasal voice answered after only two rings.

"Belden Van de Groot, please," I said.

"One moment." An electronic click was followed by muzak-on-hold.

A cockroach shot across a pile of cardboard take-out boxes. A stack of dishes sat in gray water.

"Mister Van de Groot's office." A woman's voice. Officious, precise. An I've-already-got-you-by-the-balls voice.

"I want to speak with Belden," I said.

"I'm sorry, but —"

"Let's not do it this way, okay? This is Mike Travis, Belden's brother. I'd like to speak with him *now*, please."

"I really don't think —"

"Now. Please."

"Ju— Just a moment.." She retreated into the silent power of Van de Groot Capital.

There was another click and a full two minutes of muzak. He came on the line. Harried, edgy.

"You'll never guess where I am," I said.

"Listen, I don't have time for —"

"I'm in the kitchen at the beach house," I finished.

"Oh. I see." His tone suddenly sheepish. "I can explain —"

"I doubt it. I stopped by the place this morning. You know what I found, in addition to the wreckage from a three day bender? Some burned-out jerkoff telling me to..." I took the phone away from my ear and looked over at Danny Webb. "How did you put it? 'Haul ass?' Was that it?"

Webb watched me. He was cooling off, starting to think.

"Look, Mike. I know we have an arrangement. I know you were planning on using the place, okay? But we're in the middle of an important deal with the guy, and I let him use the house for a couple weeks. Sort of a goodwill gesture. That shouldn't be too hard for you to understand."

I couldn't imagine what Danny Webb could possibly have that would interest Belden and VGC.

"No. Not difficult to understand at all, Belden. But I don't really care how important your deal is, I think you friend here is king of the shitheads. The place is trashed, and no telling what felonies have been going on in here. I want him gone."

"He's not standing *right there*, is he?" My brother sounded sick.

"Want to talk to him?"

"Oh, Jesus, Mike. You talked about him like that right in *front* of him? Oh my God. Do you have any idea how important —"

"Fill me in later. I'll put him on, and you can arrange for his departure." I handed the receiver to Danny Webb.

Webb looked at me with loathing.

"Yeah," he said into the mouthpiece. Mr. Charm.

I watched him listen, grunt periodically, nod. He finally looked over at me, tried to give me a hard look that didn't quite come off. "Yeah, okay, Belden, no hard feelings. Friday's cool. Later." He hung up.

The stairs creaked as someone descended the staircase. I turned and saw another haggard looking man in his late thirties, early forties, shirtless, wearing only a pair of faded swim trunks. He absently scratched his balls and yawned, a skinny arm draped over the shoulders of a girl that couldn't have been over seventeen. She looked stoned to the gills.

The guy looked at me, then at Webb.

"What's going on, man?" Thin nasal voice. Rock star hanger-on.

"Nothing," Webb said, annoyed.

I turned and started to leave.

"Clean this place up good, rock star," I said. "You live like a pig."

I could feel his eyes boring into my back. As I got to the door, I turned to face him again. "One more thing."

"What?"

"Get that girl back home or I'll see you do time for statutory rape."

*   *   *

OUTSIDE, I saw Tino sitting in a beat up wicker chair on the lanai in front of his house. His had been built, I guessed, in the 1930's. It was constructed of wood with a corrugated metal roof that had long since rusted to a ruddy brown. A classic Hawaiian coffee shack.

Recognition finally crossed his face, like moving from shadow to sunlight.

"Hey, Mik*aaay*! Howzit, brah?" he said as he rose unsteadily from his seat.

"How you, bruddah?" I responded in the easy pidgin so prevalent among locals.

"Long time, man! Let me look at you," he said, stopping about three feet from me and giving me a theatrical once over. "We all grown up now, huh, Mikey?" He embraced me with his thick brown arms.

"All grown up," I said.

Tino was constructed of geometric patterns. His head was a wide oval balanced on a solid square torso between broad shoulders. His neck was lost in there somewhere. He had legs like tree stumps and his whole body rocked from side to side when he walked. A thick tangle of black hair stuck up in unruly tufts, like he had just woken up. He wore only a pair of tattered blue shorts and rubber sandals.

"You look good, Mikey," he smiled and patted his bare brown stomach. "I come fat."

"Too much kaukau," I said.

"And beer," he added with a laugh. "Come sit, man. Let's talk story, yeah?"

I followed him to his house. "So where's Ruby?"

"She's workeen', man. Cleaneen' houses, yeah?" His voice inflected like a question, but it wasn't. "She be back in a while. Can you wait around? She'll be mad if she don't see you."

"I'd like to see her, too." I asked what he was doing home so late.

"Things been slow, brah. Not much work, you know? If you don't got one gover'ment job, things real slow," he shook his head sadly as he looked at the scarred wood floorboards between his feet.

"Anything I can do?" I offered.

"No, man. Thanks. We be fine."

The rattling of palm fronds sounded like rain above my head. In the distance, swells broke on the shoreline.

We spent the next hour talking, dusting off old memories, becoming friends again. He told me about becoming a father, and how strange it is to see his child grow up. Ruby and Tino had one daughter, Edita. She had just turned fifteen, and was named after Tino's mother.

But I felt there was something dark beneath the surface. Something brooding, caged. I could tell things were much tougher for him and his family than he was letting on. Maybe some trouble with his daughter. I remembered Captain Cerillo's admonition to tell Tino to stay out of trouble.

"I met Max Cerillo yesterday," I said. I watched Tino stiffen.

"Yeah? What for you wanna see him?"

"Professional courtesy. I wanted the locals to know I'm here."

"Yeah, sure. I forget you're a cop sometimes," he said almost apologetically.

"*Was* a cop. I'm retired now."

"Yeah sure. Okay."

A displaced tension hung between us.

"You sure everything's okay, Tino?"

"Look —" he started, annoyance bordering on anger colored his tone. He caught himself and re-started. "Look, Mike, everything's cool. Really. Hey, how about —"

Tino was cut off by the barking of a dog that had just rounded the corner of his house at a full run. Misjudging its own speed, his rear end slipped out from under him in a cloud of dust. The dog recovered its footing, then ran directly to Tino, all tongue and wagging tail.

"Hey, boy," Tino crooned, as he scratched behind its droopy ears. "This is 'Poi Dog'."

Poi Dog broke away from Tino to sniff curiously around me. I took the dog's face in my hands and scratched him, removing the dog's long nose from my crotch.

"Nice dog," I said. "What is he?"

"A poi dog, brah. A mutt. A little of everything."

"Stray?"

"Naw. Edita brought him back from town when he was just a puppy. Somebody was giving them away. I was kinda pissed at first, but the goddamn thing is so friendly, I couldn't stay mad. I let her keep 'im."

A dirty Japanese sedan, one hubcap missing, pulled up and parked next to my rented Mustang. A cloud of dust rolled away as the engine dieseled to a stop.

The woman was tall and slender. She leaned in to retrieve a bag of groceries, tucked it under her arm and approached the lanai where Tino and I sat. I felt Tino's discomfort immediately.

Realizing she must be Ruby, I rose from my chair. She wore short cutoff jeans and a sleeveless white cotton blouse, her lissome figure only beginning to show the effects of encroaching middle age. Dancer's legs were still well-toned, and a familiar tattoo that she had had since she was fifteen ringed her ankle. Long copper hair in a ponytail. Loose strands across her cheeks. Oversized dark glasses.

When Ruby finally recognized me, her back became rigid and she stopped in her tracks.

I approached her, smiling.

"It's been a long time, Ruby."

"Look, baby, it's Mikey Travis," Tino put in. False joviality laced his voice.

I hugged her gently, the bag of groceries perched awkwardly between us. Stepping back, my hands moved to her upper arms, and I looked her squarely in the face. Keep smiling, Travis, until you get this figured out.

I felt Ruby shudder as she broke free. She angled her head down and moved quickly to the house without so much as a word.

As she brushed past me, I noticed the lingering green and purple marks beneath her eyes.

"Tino?"

Tino looked away.

"Talk to me." I felt bile in my throat.

Tino watched the dog. "I got drunk, Mike. I don't know what the hell happened, man, but she must have pissed me off—"

"Bullshit." My hands were squeezed into fists.

"I've never been so fuckin' sorry in my life, Mikey. It's just that..." He blinked back his humiliation. "It's just that with no work for me, and Ruby having to clean houses for people..."

"Lots of people like that. They manage."

"She even cleans up after that asshole in your house three times inna last week! God, it's just too damn much some times... aw, fuck it, you wouldn't understand." He back-handed a tear as it leaked down his face.

"You been drinking a lot, Tino?"

"How the fuck do I know? How much is a lot, man?"

"You beat on your wife. *That's* a lot. That's too fucking much."

"Now you gonna judge me, eh, Mike?" He asked angrily. "Why don't you just fuck off then. Mind your own damn business, huh?"

"No hitting."

"I think I heard enough now. I said I was sorry. The fuck-een' cops came, humiliated me in front of my daughter. I said I was sorry then, too. Shit! What you all want anyway? Go on, now. Leave us be."

He turned and stalked off toward the beach. Poi Dog nipped at Tino's retreating heels.

I looked across at their front door, still standing open, wind flapping the screen. I looked at my house, shut tight against the day.

With nothing left to do, I made the drive back to Kona. I drove slow, feeling sick, realizing that things are no longer as they once were.

Hell, maybe they never were.

*   *   *

THE EASTERN sky glowed red the next morning. Sailor take warning, the saying goes. I was drinking a cup of Mango Ceylon and checking the pressure in the scuba tanks I was planning to use later with Rex and Dave.

In the salon below, my cell phone rang.

"Mike Travis," I said.

"Mr. Travis? This is Captain Cerillo from the Kona police. We spoke yesterday?"

"Yes. 'Morning, Captain —"

"There's been some trouble, Mr. Travis. We need to meet." Cop voice.

Something ugly washed down my body in a rush of ice.

"What kind of trouble?"

"There's been a murder at your house at Honaunau. Multiple murders, actually."

"Jesus —"

"I'll pick you up at the Kona pier," Cerillo interrupted. "We'll ride down together."

"Give me ten minutes," I said and hung up.

Two days in the islands and death had already found me.

Check out these other fine titles by
Durban House at your local book store.

Exceptional Books
by
Exceptional Writers

TUNNEL RUNNER by Richard Sand.

Tunnel Runner is a fast, deadly espionage thriller peopled with quirky and most times vicious characters. It tells of a dark world where murder is committed and no one is brought to account; where loyalties exist side by side with lies and extreme violence.

Ashman "the hunter, the hero, the killer" is a denizen of that world who awakens to find himself paralyzed in a mental hospital. He escapes and seeks vengeance, confronting this old friends, the Pentagon, the Mafia, and a mysterious general who is covering up the attack on TWA Flight 800.

People begin to die. There are shoot-outs and assassinations. A woman is blown up in her bathtub.

Ashman is cunning and ruthless as he moves through the labyrinth of deceit, violence, and suspicion. He is a tunnel runner, a ferret in the hole, who needs the danger to survive and hates them who have made him so.

It is this peculiar combination of ruthlessness and vulnerability that redeems Ashman as he goes for those who want him dead. Join him.

OPAL EYE DEVIL by John Lewis

From the teeming wharves of Shanghai to the stately offices of New York and London, schemes are hammered out to bankrupt opponents, wreck inventory, and dynamite oil wells. It is the age of the Robber Baron --- a time when powerful men lie, steal, cheat, and even kill in their quest for power.

Sweeping us back to the turn of the twentieth century, John Lewis weaves an extraordinary tale about the brave men and women who risk everything as the discovery of oil rocks the world.

Follow Eric Gradek's rise from Northern Star's dark cargo hold to the pinnacle of high stakes gambling for unrivaled riches.

Aided by his beautiful wife, Katheryn, and the devoted Tong-Po, Eric fights for his dream and for revenge against the man who left him for dead aboard Northern Star.

MR. IRRELEVANT by Jerry Marshall.

Sports writer Paul Tenkiller and pro-football player Chesty Hake have been roommates for eight career seasons. Paul's Choctaw background of poverty and his gambling on sports, and Hake's dark memories of his mother being killed are the forces which will make their friendship go horribly wrong.

Chesty Hake, the last man chosen in the draft, has been dubbed Mr. Irrelevant. By every yardstick, he should not be playing pro football. But, because of his heart and high threshold for pain, he preservers.

Paul Tenkiller has been on a gravy train because of Hake's generosity. Gleaning information vital to gambling on football, his relationship with Hake is at once loyal and deceitful.

Then during his eighth and final season, Hake slides into paranoia and Tenkiller is caught up in the dilemma. But Paul is behind the curve, and events spiral out of his control, until the bloody end comes in murder and betrayal.

Coming January, 2001 from
Durban House Publishing Company

DEATH OF A HEALER by Paul Henry Young

Paul Henry Young's compelling tale Death of a Healer clearly places him into the spotlight as one of America's premier writers of medical thrillers. The Story stunningly illuminates the darker side of the medical world in a way nonfiction could never accomplish.

Death of a Healer chronicles the lifelong journey of Jake Gibson, M.D., diehard romanticist and surgeon extraordinaire, as he struggles to preserve his professional oath against the avarice and abuse of power so prevalent in present-day America.

Follow Jake as he runs headfirst into a group of sinister medical and legal practitioners determined to destroy his beloved profession. Events begin spinning out of control when Jake uncovers a nationwide plot by hospital executives to eliminate certain patient groups in order to improve the bottom line.

With the lives of his family on the line, Jake invokes a self-imposed banishment as a missionary doctor and rediscovers his lifelong obsession to be a trusted physician.

Death of a Healer is a masterfully constructed suspense novel; packed with the kind of gritty authenticity only a gifted writer can portray.